PRAISE FOR ANTHONY OLIVER AND HIS INIMITABLE MYSTERY SERIES

"Mr. Oliver writes with a nice down-to-earth touch."

The New York Times

"Oliver is a Welshman who gave up acting for the antique business. . . . He is a sell-out for entertainment."

Chicago Tribune

"The tone is mild, the tempo is moderate, and, what is most impressive, Mr. Oliver has both the artistry and the patience to give even the least of his characters a personality all his or her own."

The New Yorker

"A skillful and sensitive writer."

The New York Times Book Review

"Pure delight for fans of English mysteries."

Mem[illegible]mercial Appeal

Also by Anthony Oliver
Published by Fawcett Crest Books:

THE PEW GROUP

THE PROPERTY OF A LADY

THE ELBERG COLLECTION

COVER-UP

Anthony Oliver

FAWCETT CREST • NEW YORK

A Fawcett Crest Book
Published by Ballantine Books

Library of Congress Catalog Card Number: 86-29195

ISBN 0-449-21466-4

This edition published by arrangement with Doubleday & Company, Inc.

Manufactured in the United States of America

First Ballantine Books Edition: July 1988

ONE

In just over an hour and twenty minutes Joseph Greenwood would be dead.

The sleet on the windscreen could turn into snow, he thought miserably, and that was the last thing he wanted in a lonely lane miles from anywhere with no sign of a building, nor of anyone he could stop and ask the way. Indigestion nagged at him and he felt in the glove compartment for the peppermints again. He tried to remember how long ago it was when he'd last eaten and gave it up.

The day had been like one of a hundred others on the road, stopping at all his usual places and eating a sandwich when he could, and only then if he found a pub open at the right time. If things had gone as he'd planned he would have been well on the way back to London by now. But that was before he'd seen the photograph. He thought ruefully of the hot bath he had planned before being entertained at one of the best restaurants in London. Too late now, at least he'd been lucky to find a phone-box that was working and cancel the appointment. You didn't upset buyers if you could help it, and if this turned out to be a wild goose chase, well, it wouldn't be the first time.

Another mile, and it was snowing in earnest now, so that the signpost was barely legible. One arm said "Wangford half a mile" and the other "Warren Lane." Warren Lane—

that was the address he'd seen in the phone book, and almost at once he saw a name on the gate of a house in the light of his headlamps. Fox House. Time for action.

The young man who answered his ring was big, nearly filling the doorway, but behind him Greenwood could see a woman standing in the hall.

"Good evening. I'm sorry to disturb you. I would have telephoned but I'm afraid I ran out of coins. I wonder if I might speak to Miss Varley? My name is Greenwood. Joseph Greenwood. I'm a friend of Mr. Gough, the estate agent in Flaxfield."

His best voice, well practiced, polite, low-toned with a hint of shyness. It seemed to reassure her and she came and stood beside the man in the doorway. Not that she need be afraid of strangers, he thought, not with a young giant to protect her.

"Come in, do. God, what a night! Shut the door, Harry, or we'll have a snow-drift in the hall. Come in to the fire. I'm Victoria Varley, Mr. Fellows is a friend of mine. You'd best take your coat off."

A decent room, nothing special—chintz, poor paintings, a log fire, the sort of fire people lived in the country for. In a corner, out of the light, some pottery stood on a small table and a canvas was propped against the wall. He carefully avoided looking at them and accepted a sherry. He remembered his father's advice and avoided charm. Quiet sincerity, with the slightest hint of knowledgeable authority, underlined by his well-tailored suit with the money evenly distributed in all the pockets so that it wouldn't spoil the cut. There was another reason for that, too—he needn't reveal how much he always carried with him.

Small talk first—the weather and gratitude for the fire, reserved appreciation of the cheap sherry and his long-standing friendship with Mr. Gough. She ought not to be too difficult. He didn't know about the man, or indeed what the relationship was. There was something vaguely familiar about her, something in the back of his memory that he couldn't place. Not beautiful but a face you felt you should know. He sipped his drink and tried to place her. The young man didn't join them at the fire, but busied himself with the bottles on the drinks table. Greenwood saw her catch his eye and watched him leave the room with a few words of excuse. A rough accent and rough clothes, a rough friend for this elegant woman, who was clasping her knee with manicured hands and waiting for Greenwood to explain his visit.

"Thank you, that was most welcome. You're very kind but I won't keep you. Let me try and be as brief as I can." He handed her a card which said, "Fronefield and Greenwood—Fine Art." "I feel rather like one of those ghastly people you read about who knock on doors and try to buy antiques for pennies!"

It was always sensible to put the worst case first. Before they could suspect it for themselves.

"So you're not a knocker or a runner or a con man?"

Her smile took some of the sting out of it but it would have been better, he thought, if she had just smiled. Again he had that nagging feeling at the illusive memory of her face. The smile, too. Not in a sale-room, please God. That would be too unkind. A country dealer? Or one of those boring legions of enthusiastic amateurs who were invading the auctions more and more? The furniture and the paintings on the walls reassured him. No dealer, not even an amateur, would buy rubbish like that.

His answering smile, she thought, was quite good. Patiently good-humoured, a joke shared. An expensive suit, and his business card was engraved, not printed. At least with Harry in the house she felt safe. In the house but not in the room—there was no need to share everything, not even with Harry.

The sherry seemed to have helped the indigestion more than the peppermint, or perhaps it was excitement and the memory of the photograph.

"I told you I knew Mr. Gough. He sometimes has local sales, house contents, nothing special but we cover them if they sound at all promising." "We" sounded better than "I," a reputable firm going diligently about its business.

"Not just yet, Harry, we're talking business. I'll call you if I want you."

The young man's face showed no resentment and he left the room again, this time closing the door. Some kind of servant, then. Or a lover? Both perhaps, although she must be quite a bit older.

"The weather has been so rotten he's had to delay his spring sale," Greenwood said.

"Afraid the punters wouldn't turn up." She nodded. "That sounds like Gough."

She could have put it more politely. After all, he had claimed the man as a friend.

"I went to see a Mrs. Teasdale. He is going to sell a cottage for her but he hasn't removed the contents yet. I believe you know her?"

"Minnie Teasdale. She sometimes cleans for me. I knew her father, too. He used to help with the garden here. I liked him. I bought some of his things from her and you want to see them. Am I right?"

"Quite right. She mentioned a Toby Jug with a black face."

"You mean this."

Whatever age she was, he thought, as he rose and followed her to the table in the corner, she was not too old to look good in jeans. She'd kept her figure and she walked well. But there were more important things to think about.

The Toby was a pleasant surprise. It could have been any old rubbish with a face blackened by smoke and dirt; God knows they'd made enough of them through the years. This one wasn't rubbish, though. You couldn't mistake it. Ralph Wood, about 1770, and as right as rain. Well, that was an added bonus. He tried hard to look at the canvas propped against the wall without turning his head away from the Toby and felt the blood thump in his chest. The silly-born bitch, why did she have to shove the painting *there*, of all places, instead of in the light where he could see it properly.

"May I?" He took the pottery reverently in his hands and carried it to the fire and into the light. "Miss Varley, have you any idea how valuable this is?"

He could see that it wasn't what she had expected. Good—that was encouraging and nice to see the usual reactions in her expression. Surprise, followed by excitement, curiosity, and greed.

"They were her father's; she wanted me to have something of his to remember him by. I told you, I was fond of him. He helped in the garden until he got past it. I gave her something, of course. She was perfectly satisfied. I wouldn't dream of—"

"Please! Of course not. How indeed could you have known." He placed it carefully on the mantelshelf and stood back to admire it. "It's called 'The Collier,' " he said, "or sometimes 'The Miner,' for obvious reasons." He could have been addressing an attentive audience on a guided tour in a museum. "Late eighteenth century, one of the best things made by Ralph Wood, Senior, and much sought after. The last one to come up at auction fetched eight hundred pounds, if my memory serves me right."

It was true. Nice to be honest, a pleasant change from

some of the rubbish he'd praised in his day, and bought, too. It didn't really matter what it was; a sprat to catch—not a mackerel but, God willing, a whale. He'd once paid one hundred pounds for a Woolworth corkscrew.

He glanced at his watch. "I'm not very happy about that snow. I'm sure you don't want to be landed with an uninvited visitor! Let's see, my coat is in the hall, isn't it? I really am most grateful to you for letting me see it. I'm sure you don't want to sell it but do please keep my card and let me know if you ever do."

It was all too quick for her liking. At least the man was honest enough or he wouldn't be leaving, snow or no snow. It was exciting to have bought a bargain but frustrating not to have the pleasure of savouring it with an expert. He was already reaching for his coat in the hall.

"You said the last one fetched eight hundred pounds at auction? Do you think this one is worth that, too?"

His smile as he walked back into the room with his overcoat on his arm was the smile of a kind father indulging a pleading child with one last fairy story. In front of the mantelshelf he said, thoughtfully, "Your old gentleman must have had a good eye, Miss Varley; either that or luck. Oh yes, I should think so. A bit of a chip on the hat, but I shouldn't expect that to matter too much. Auctions can vary a lot, of course. Demand changes for certain things. I'm a picture man, really. I could advise you more accurately about paintings."

He looked at his watch again, discreetly, as if not wishing to appear rude. "Why not take it up to London? Any of the big auction rooms would be happy to advise you, I'm sure, and sell it for you, too, if you wanted to take your chance on the market. Mention my name, if you like. Tell them to put it into one of their important pottery sales. It might be worth waiting for that, say, six months or so? You'd have to pay their charges, of course. A bit of a gamble but gambling can be fun, can't it? I might even bid for it myself—if I'm still in the market by then."

"Why shouldn't you be?" She hoped that she had only imagined the sharpness in her voice.

"At the moment I have a client who wants one." His shoulders lifted apologetically. "Collectors are strange people," he said sadly. "They can blow hot and cold, I'm afraid."

"Would you pay eight hundred pounds for it?"

He put his overcoat on the arm of a chair and turned to the mantelshelf again. Always a delicate moment, the crunch, and it was never the same twice. This was more difficult than some. He hadn't even seen the damn picture properly yet, only a bloody-awful photograph that Mrs. Teasdale had shown him. Now, here, for a snatched moment in a dark corner, the thing itself. It would be fatal to ask her to show it to him. She should have risen to the bait when he'd told her that he was an expert on paintings. Keep calm and hang on. Even if he was wrong about the picture, the jug was certainly all right. The market for English pottery was growing fast and getting better every year. He wouldn't lose. It was nerve-racking, but hadn't he said himself that gambling could be fun?

"Yes, I would. That's why I came, of course, but I'm glad you asked. We are rather an old-fashioned firm, Miss Varley. I wouldn't have felt happy unless I'd told you its potential value and advised you of the possibility of selling it at auction. Who knows, you might find something else for us one day. I can't give you a cheque, I'm afraid. I always seem to use more of them than I bargained for on buying-trips. I can give you cash, if that's all right?"

The young man she'd called Harry Fellows came in carrying a heavy basket of logs without any apparent effort. "It's stopped snowing but you'll need these. I'll get some more from the shed before I go,'' he said.

''Thank you, Harry.''

He stacked the logs tidily in the hearth and they watched him in silence until he closed the door behind him. Greenwood sensed that he should leave the money until they were alone. He produced a modest roll of fifty-pound notes from a pocket. It held twenty notes and there were other rolls in other pockets. He put his glasses on to count. Sometimes the sight of money, the seeming finality of business accomplished, could help to bridge the gap he so badly wanted to cross. Not easy, this time. He counted the notes as slowly as he could, smoothing them when they were old, with folded corners. He had already prepared his first casual reference to the canvas in the corner, when he saw her walk over to it and bring it into the light.

''You said you thought the old man had a good eye. He was an artist, too, you know. An amateur, of course, but I rather liked this one. What do you think of it?''

TWO

Joseph Greenwood took the painting from her without any haste, allowing his face to light up immediately with the smile of an expert who has recognised an old friend.

''Ah! One of those.'' Thank God she had said amateur herself.

"It's not good? Not worth anything?"

"Everything," he reproved her gently, "is worth something. The amateurs of today, after all, will be the primitives of the next century and probably collected. Even today some collectors like them. You'd be surprised."

"How much do you think it's worth?"

Finally, the big question, and the most important. The one you had to get right. Too little and she might think she'd rather keep it for herself. Too much and it might give her ideas about getting a second opinion, taking it to a sale-room even. The very thought of it brought on the indigestion again.

The light in the room was very bad and he longed to shove the canvas right underneath the reading lamp and get his glass on it, but greedy women weren't complete fools and you didn't do that with a painting by an amateur. Only this wasn't painted by an amateur. It couldn't be. He'd seen the rest of the old man's work all over the walls of his cottage, ghastly things, even painted on paper, some of them, and framed with passe-partout. But this was different—even the frame was in period. It was right, it had to be. The style alone was enough, even without examining it closely. And then, there was the name of the village where the old man had lived: Wangford.

Joseph put the canvas down at the side of an armchair out of her line of sight and delicately dusted his hands together as he walked back to the Toby Jug and ran his finger lightly over the glaze. "Wonderful," he murmured appreciatively, glad of an excuse to use the word openly. "Quite wonderful."

"You didn't say what you thought the picture was worth?"

He took his eyes away from the mantelshelf reluctantly.

"The picture? Oh well, you know I don't want to appear rude, but, you see, it depends. In a sale-room? Frankly, nothing. Ten pounds perhaps? That kind of price, even if they accepted it, which is doubtful. If you knew someone who liked that sort of thing, that would be different, of course. There are such people, as I told you. Not many, but they do exist. It's a question of finding them.''

''And how much would they pay for something like that?''

They never gave up, thank God. He was surprised that the light laugh he always saved for the end-game like this sounded more forced than usual. He was tired and he probably needed food, although his hunger was deeper than that. He let the laugh die and fall into a smile. It was the father again, only this time giving away forbidden sweets.

''Not much; a hundred, two hundred, if the man's a rich fool.''

''Do you know any rich fools?''

''I really don't want to buy it, you know, '' he said apologetically. ''I'd honestly rather leave it.'' Dangerous to risk too long a pause but it was important to make it believable. He let his eyes turn back to the Toby Jug. ''But I'm being churlish. I wouldn't like to have missed this Toby Jug.''

When at last he did look at her, he pretended to interpret the fierce greed in her face as if it were the endearing pleading of an attractive young woman, amusing and difficult to resist. He sighed. At the table, he gathered together the notes he had been counting and allowed himself a look at his watch in earnest.

''Let's hope I shan't need any more petrol on my way back! You'll find it comes to a round thousand. You are a very persuasive lady, Miss Varley.'' He resisted the temptation to call her a young lady. Keep it believable; she wasn't a fool. ''Could you find a little bit of newspaper for the Toby Jug? It doesn't matter about the painting.''

''I'll ask Harry. There should be some in the kitchen.''

When the pain came he was alone in the room. Like the indigestion, it started in the centre of his chest. Only worse, much worse. Tight and crushing, it spread without mercy into his neck and down his arms. He thought he was going to die and he was right.

When they came back into the room he was lying on the floor and beyond any help.

Dr. Benjamin Lamb sat in the bar of Norland's Hotel in Mayfair and waited for his companion to join him. His name wasn't Lamb and he wasn't a doctor, but the Americans seemed to like it. It suited his English accent and he hadn't lived in New York for long before he discovered that they were more impressed by a medical degree than the military rank he had often assumed in England. A doctor who preferred to advise rich American collectors and to impress them with his knowledge of British paintings was someone who had caught their imagination. They would have been less impressed if they had known that he had been a male nurse in the British Army and had been in prison for manslaughter. He was lucky, the judge had told him, that the charge hadn't been murder. A model prisoner, he had earned full remission, made good use of the prison library, and on his release had gone to America with a false passport. There, in their fabulous museums and with their helpful curators and librarians, he had diligently increased his knowledge but had never again pursued his old skill as a robber of fine paintings, a man not averse to using violence if it was unavoidable. In America he had been very careful. He had no desire to get himself a police record as he had in England. Those days, he told himself, were over. You didn't need violence to rob people, there was no law against big profits. It was, he told himself, a question of supply and demand and called for a high degree of expertise on both sides of the Atlantic. The art boom was very big business; Dr. Lamb had done well and over the years worked hard to supply his collectors who lacked knowledge but not money. England was still a treasure-house, if you looked hard enough, but the money was in America.

The telephone call from Joseph Greenwood, cancelling their dinner appointment, had intrigued him as it had been intended it should. The expensive dinner in Norland's over-priced restaurant was to have been a business gesture, to acknowledge Joseph's usefulness in the past, not to celebrate anything on this trip, which had proved to be very dull and unproductive. Until now.

"Hi," Mrs. Lamb greeted, and joined him.

She wasn't Mrs. Lamb either but they found it convenient to travel as husband and wife. She moved and sat like a professional tennis player between games. That indeed was what she had been until too many defeats had convinced her that she was in the wrong game and she had fallen back on an arts degree from an obscure school in Ohio which had optimistically decided to call itself a university. She had met Benjamin at an even more obscure art gallery on Long Island where she was working as a receptionist. Intrigued by his money, his accent, and his easy amorality, April Schittski had needed little persuasion to join him as a doubles partner. Benjamin had made his offer shortly after seeing her eject an unwelcome visitor to the gallery, who had demanded money at gunpoint. Her backhand had always been one of April's better strokes and she had broken the gunman's neck. A lover and a bodyguard in time of need, Benjamin considered, was an admirable combination.

"I guess I'm all packed," she said, "and I've checked the early flight tomorrow. Where's the Greenwood guy? And when do we eat?" She transferred a saucerful of toasted peanuts to the palm of her hand.

"Joseph has been delayed and we can eat as soon as you've finished eating. And you can cancel the flight; we shall be staying for a while."

* * *

"It stands to reason," Mrs. Thomas said. "Nobody likes to find a complete stranger sitting on their lavatory, especially if he's dead."

Her friend, John Webber, nodded pacifically.

High tea in Mrs. Thomas's kitchen was not a good time to disagree with her and he addressed himself to his kippered herring with keen anticipation. If you chose to live in the chill of East Anglia then you thanked God for the compensations, and of these, high on his list, was the luxury of a kipper from Great Yarmouth. He had no intention of spoiling his meal and she had the grace to let him finish it in peace. Not for the first time, he admired the restraint of this dumpy little Welsh woman with the curiosity of a foraging squirrel, who could cook like an angel and allowed him to enjoy his food with dignity.

"Natural causes," she sighed when eventually she poured their second cups of tea.

"A massive coronary," Webber said firmly. "You can't argue with the evidence of a qualified pathologist."

She wasn't going to argue with Webber either—as a retired policeman he knew what he was talking about.

"Had you expected the poor man to be full of cyanide?" He smiled. He had nearly said "Hoped," but changed his mind. Just be grateful that they lived in Flaxfield, where people still died from natural causes and where daffodils were blooming on the first day of spring.

"All the same," she said, "it doesn't make sense."

With only the slightest feeling of apprehension, he watched her carefully remove the bones from the remains of the kippers on the plates. However distracted, she was not likely to forget her cat.

"People do die of sudden heart attacks. It often happens in the lavatory, too. Not very nice but there it is." He stifled a belch with a wheeze of quiet satisfaction, relaxing in the safety of the verdict of the coroner's court. She couldn't argue with that. "So why doesn't it make sense?" he said.

"A total stranger turns up at a lonely house miles from anywhere, asks if he can use the lavatory, and the woman lets him in without a murmur?"

"You heard her give evidence. He was well dressed and well spoken, it was an expensive looking car, and he was obviously taken short. Come on, Lizzie, be fair. Unless she wanted a disaster on the doorstep, what else could she have done?"

"Lonely roads, miles of fields—why couldn't he have gone behind a bush?"

"You are naughty, you know. A good counsel would tear you to pieces in court! They're keen on facts."

"Those are facts."

"Yes, there are fields, but Warren Lane has very steep banks and high hedges, and on top of that it was snowing hard. He could have used the ditch, I suppose, but Fox House isn't the only house around there. Believe it or not, most people would be quite embarrassed to be seen in a lane with their trousers down in a blizzard."

"They never were down. He was sitting on the loo properly dressed, and that is a fact."

"That's what inquests are for. You heard what the doctor said: people feeling unwell before a heart attack often think that they need to use a lavatory. Greenwood could have been in exactly that condition."

"Why didn't he lock the door? Most people do."

"No time."

She was silent, remembering the cold room of the coroner's court, with the bored faces impatient for the foregone conclusion. Webber relaxed and allowed himself to think of the coloured seed catalogues and the holiday brochures waiting for him at home. If she were a child, he reflected, she would probably be diagnosed as hyperactive. Perhaps she had been. Wales must seem very dull without her. Dull and peaceful.

During the next few days the temperature grudgingly acknowledged the season and edged cautiously upwards. The last of the snow shrank into the hedgerows, splashed with rain and mud. It could not be called warm but Mrs. Thomas got her bicycle out of the garden shed and oiled it. It was a surer sign of the approach of April than any weather forecast. The stubborn buds on the trees were not yet out, but Mrs. Thomas was.

Her daughter, Doreen, and her son-in-law, Jimmy Trottwood—Betsey to his friends—stood in the window of their village antique shop and watched her wheeled approach with mixed feelings. Betsey liked Mrs. Thomas. He did not always approve of her clothes but had long since given up trying to impose his own ideas upon her. Perhaps she was right after all, he thought. There was something to be said for her appalling taste; it was always practical and could often give some indication of the mood she was in. It could even, although this was more difficult, indicate her immediate destination.

Today, with a steady rain falling, she had bowed to expediency and wore a quilted Husky jacket with corduroy trousers tucked into green wellington boots. Had she not opted for a fisherman's sou'wester, to which she had pinned a daffodil, she would not have disgraced a shooting party at Sandringham or Balmoral.

Her relationship with her daughter had never been easy, but she returned her son-in-law's affection and respected his gentle, feminine nature and his usefulness as a reliable source of local gossip.

"One day," Doreen told her, "you'll kill yourself on that bike, the way the wheels wobble."

"Safe as sitting on the lav, safer than some. What do you know about Victoria Varley?"

"Mam! You're dripping all over the floor."

"Only clean rain," Mrs. Thomas said, and continued shaking the sou'wester gently to avoid damaging her daffodil. "I shan't stop long, just for a cup of tea, perhaps? And a biscuit or something!" she called to Doreen's ungracious back.

"Victoria Varley? Not much more than it said in *The Gazette*. She is an actress, that's true, but more like forty-five than thirty-five. I can remember her on television years ago but she doesn't do much now—small parts and the odd bit in a commercial. There's a flat in London, I think. She rents the house in Warren Lane. I've got an idea she's married but he never comes down; perhaps he isn't around anymore. She's been in here once or twice."

"Did she buy anything?"

"Too mean," said Doreen, carrying in a tray heavy with one of her cakes.

"She always says she's forgotten her cheque book." Betsey laughed. "She's a J.P.—Just Pricing. Likes to keep an eye on the market. She's got quite a good eye, but no real knowledge. Beady is as good a word for her as any. A bit beady-eyed."

"She made him deliver a chair on appro," Doreen sniffed, pouring the tea before it had drawn properly, "and then said it didn't suit her. Cheeky cat!"

"She never intended to buy it," Betsey said with grudging admiration. "It was an excuse. She wanted a free valuation for all her bits and pieces."

Mrs. Thomas was chewing a mouthful of her daughter's

soggy cake with disbelief and forced herself to swallow it. "You didn't fall for it?"

"I offered to do it for fifteen pounds and she said she'd think about it." He beamed with pleasure at the memory of Victoria Varley's frustration.

"You're a fool," his wife told him. "You let people twist you round their little finger. Questions, questions, just picking your brain for free information. Three miles down that narrow lane and caught in a herd of cows on the way back."

"I'm not very good with cows."

His red crew-cut wig, Mrs. Thomas thought, should have made him more than a match for a herd of cows. But, far from making him look aggressive, it sat uneasily on the sandy nest of his own hair making him look only gentle and sad.

"Any boy-friends?" she asked.

"People talk, but no more than usual down here."

Neither Betsey nor Doreen were surprised by her cross examination. The fact that a stranger had succumbed to a heart attack, in circumstances which had in no way aroused the slightest interest in anyone except Mrs. Thomas, seemed perfectly natural to both of them.

"What is her house like inside? Would it have been worth a valuation?"

"Not really. She's made it look quite pleasant, but nothing good—horse brasses, and lamps made out of farmyard junk. You know the sort of thing; a bit like those articles in the women's magazines: 'Why not get a farmer friend to lend you an old cartwheel.' "

"He was an art dealer from London. He had a shop in Kensington Church Street. What could he want down here?"

"I don't know. Kensington Church Street is very grand. But I've never heard of him." Betsey was polite but it was past the time for his afternoon nap.

"Why not try Mr. Gough at the estate agents?" Doreen

said, cleaning the tea-things. "He might have a house sale coming up, but nothing worthwhile or we would have heard about it."

For once Doreen had made a sensible suggestion and her mother was grateful and showed it. She adjusted her sou'wester and kissed her daughter on the cheek. "I mustn't keep you. Ta for the tea. Lovely cake, nice and firm."

THREE

Gough and Groucher's office at the end of the High Street was deserted and she was shown into Mr. Gough's private room by a young woman with no bust and large hips. He had had time to hide his crossword, leaving only an impressive clutter of documents on his desk. He completed an unnecessary sentence in a notebook before looking up and brushing aside her apologies.

"Not at all, not at all, glad of the chance of a break. I was about to have tea. Have you had tea?"

"No," she said firmly. "That would be very nice."

He knew Mrs. Thomas of old. He did not dislike her but he regarded her with cautious respect. The young woman produced two large mugs of tea and Mrs. Thomas had time to edge the conversation to her chosen subject.

"Ah yes, sad indeed, sad indeed. I imagine the poor man must have been on his way home to London. Very distressing. He had a fine eye. The art world will miss him." Mr.

Gough liked to present himself and the firm of Gough and Groucher as being very near the hub of the world at auction.

"You knew him, of course?"

"We know them all," he said importantly.

"Do you know why he came down here?"

He leaned back in his chair and sipped his tea, the button of his jacket straining against his stomach, and considered the question. He produced a packet of ginger biscuits from a tin on the mantelshelf. It was all over and done with now, he thought, and even if he had given evidence at the inquest it wouldn't have altered anything. The man could have dropped dead anywhere in the whole of England. Mr. Gough disliked officialdom with its time-wasting self-importance and needless enquiries into people's private affairs. The thought of hanging about in draughty municipal corridors only to give a pompous coroner quite useless and unnecessary information had not appealed to him. Here in his private office, in command of his own ship, it was another matter. However much people deplored her inquisitive nature, this woman had shown deference and due respect, even apologising for intruding, without an appointment, into the office hours of a busy man. He moved a pile of papers an unnecessary fraction to the left and was lured by the luxury of a captive and attentive audience. So attentive and still, indeed, that a drop of rainwater hung suspended and undisturbed on the lowest petal-tip of her daffodil.

His fingers touched together delicately over the desk. "Why was he down here? It is indeed curious how things turn out. A busy man like Mr. Greenwood, and a country lane near Wangford. One cannot, of course, blame oneself in the smallest degree and yet, indirectly, one might say that I myself was responsible."

The rain drop fell with satisfying accuracy into the very centre of her mug of tea.

* * *

By the time she left his office, the drizzle had turned into a shower and then, as if enjoying itself, into a steady downpour. It would have been sensible to have gone home, she thought, but then decided that she might make Webber a cup of tea. Her capacity for tea was impressive.

She found him surrounded by his brochures, with the coloured photographs promising him riotous herbaceous borders and cruises among the islands of Greece. A holiday, she conceded, was an excusable dream and not too time-consuming. His garden took up a disproportionate amount of his energy. Each seasonal blaze of bloom throughout the year she secretly considered a flamboyant testament to a wasted talent. Even in high summer she preferred her own garden, a desert wilderness of neglect where a cat could hide and dream and hunt.

"In what way could Gough be responsible?" Webber asked.

"He likes to get the highest prices he can for things in his auctions. He makes sure that London dealers know the dates of his sales."

"Very sensible."

"Betsey and Doreen don't think so."

"Well, they wouldn't, would they? So he wrote to Greenwood?"

"He likes to give the impression that he knows everyone intimately. It's not quite like that, he just sends out photostats of his pre-sale notices. The snow has been so bad this year that he hasn't been able to collect all the stuff he was going to put into his spring sale, so he postponed it. Some dealers were told and some he forgot. Greenwood was one. He came down to view. Gough wasn't in the office when he called. The girl there gave him one or two places where he could view the contents. One of them seemed to interest him."

Webber tried to imagine himself sunbathing on a nudist beach near St. Tropez and failed.

"Not the Varley woman? She wasn't selling?"

"No, nothing to do with her. A cottage and contents; an old man had died."

Webber was sitting at an open-air restaurant on the island of Paxos. He was sharing a table with a girl of nineteen. There were candles and the lights of the cruise ship in the waters of the harbour. He was cracking the claws of her lobster for her while she poured him a glass of retsina.

"Well, then," he said, conscious of the eyes of his tea-time companion in Flaxfield, "no mystery. He felt ill on the way back to London and we know the rest."

"Except that Victoria Varley's house is nowhere near the London road. Miles out of his way."

"Perhaps he got lost."

"He'd been down before. He was on Gough's list, remember."

Webber politely abandoned his brochure.

"A pleasant drive back, perhaps? A gentle amble through England's green and pleasant land?"

"East Anglia? In March and snowing?" She pulled on her cycling gloves and smiled at him without rancour. If he wasn't interested, he wasn't interested. Poor old thing, perhaps he was ageing prematurely. She studied the brochure over his shoulder with interest.

"Quite right, stick to wine. You couldn't drink the water, that's for sure, or eat the lobster either. The Mediterranean is the dirtiest sea in the world, it was in the paper. Pretty girl though, lovely big mouth, sets her teeth off."

"You think he was going to see the Varley woman?"

"Don't ask me, someone in Wangford might know. I thought I'd ask. No harm in asking."

* * *

The rain was stubborn, bad for her varicose veins. Nevertheless, when it didn't let up for days, she resorted to her pink elastic stockings and prepared to cycle through the four miles of muddy lanes to Wangford. She was too proud to ask Webber to drive her but delighted when Betsey found himself offering to drive her over. From the girl in Gough's office she got the address of the cottage in Wangford which had interested Joseph Greenwood.

"You say you've never heard of him?" she said.

Betsey shook his head and pulled the car in close to the hedge to let a farm tractor squeeze past. "Fronefield and Greenwood, it said in *The Gazette*, but there was no photograph of him. 'Fine Art' sounds like paintings. I get loads of London dealers in the shop. He could well have been in at some time or other. They like sales best, where they can ring the prices."

"I've read about rings, but I've never been clear about how they work," she said.

"Dealers in a ring agree not to bid against each other. It keeps the price down. Only one of them bids for a lot and gets it cheap. When the auction is over they meet somewhere privately and auction it again between themselves. It's illegal but difficult to stop. It happens all the time. Dealers in a ring pretend that they don't see anything wrong in it. They argue that you can't expect friends not to get together."

"They don't sound very nice people."

Betsey slowed down to ease the car through an unpleasant lake of mud and cow dung. "You've met some of them in the shop." She looked so shocked he couldn't help laughing at the outrage on her face. "Respectable country dealers, my dear. Wives, children, black Labradors, and regular churchgoers, every Easter and Christmas. If you do buy something they want and refuse to settle with them, they'll try and damage it in some way before you can collect it at the end of the sale. If they can't manage that, they'll let your tyres down in the car-park. You can't prove anything, of course." He sighed. "Sometimes I think I'm only honest because I'm such a coward."

The road opened up and the hedges gave way to isolated houses and cottages on the outskirts of the village.

"I expect I've made it sound worse than it is," he said cheerfully. "Here we are, by the look of it. Oh dear, what a day! I hope we can find the cottage; I don't fancy traipsing round in this rain."

"Pull up by here. That looks like it to me, the one with Gough's board outside."

The cottage was semi-detached and the curtains looked dirty and neglected. In the patch of garden, nailed to a gnarled and ancient tree, Gough and Groucher's sign announced that it had been sold. Betsey switched off the engine and without it the rain drumming on the roof of the car sounded unnaturally loud. He had long ago given up trying to work out any plans she might have in mind, suspecting rightly that she made them up as she went along. His offer to drive her had not been entirely unselfish; he was curious about the cottage and its contents but, unlike so many in his trade, he was a shy man and not a great knocker-on-doors. He had faith in his mother-in-law. Sold or not, if anyone could get in, then, without doubt, Lizzie could.

"What now?" he asked with interest.

The rain bounced in the road, a public telephone box on the corner gleamed red and deserted under the dripping trees. The cottage next door looked deserted, too, but the curtains were cleaner and she had already seen one of them twitch.

"Just keep close and say nothing. I'll knock next door and see what happens."

The door opened readily enough and the woman didn't look hostile. A bit suspicious, but then most people in Suffolk were that, she thought. In Wales it would have been easier. You hardly ever had to confront a stranger there because you knew everyone. Any one of a dozen excuses could get you safely over the threshold.

"If it's about next door," the woman said, "I'm afraid you're too late, it's gone." The suspicion was still in her eyes and around her mouth.

Mrs. Thomas saw her best card and played it. "Sold through them?" She nodded at the board nailed to the apple tree.

"That's right, Mr. Gough over to Flaxfield."

"Another one!" Mrs. Thomas sighed significantly to Betsey.

It could simply have been a tribute to the industry of Gough and Groucher but the tone of her voice suggested at least three other meanings.

"It doesn't matter," she said to the woman. "I believe the old gentleman who owned it is dead anyway, isn't he?"

"That's right, seven weeks last Thursday."

Mrs. Thomas nodded sadly and took Betsey's arm with every appearance of leaving.

"You'd best come in," the woman said, opening the door wider. "It belonged to my Dad. I'm his daughter."

FOUR

Keep close and say nothing, Betsey decided, was good advice, and, since he had no idea of the line Mrs. Thomas would take, there was not much else he could do. He would have felt even more uncomfortable if he had known that she herself was as yet ignorant of her best approach. She was an opportunist, strategy was not her strongest suit, but as a tactician she could seldom be faulted.

In the short time it took to introducc herself and her son-in-law, and to express concern for their muddy shoes on the woman's carpet, she applied herself to the problem with diligence. The cottage was small and presumably a mirror image of her father's next door. The living-room took up most of the ground floor, the furnishing was modern and cheap, and although the rain made the place dark and cold, there was no fire. The single bulb in the ceiling light was low-powered and did little to lighten the gloom.

Mean, Mrs. Thomas thought with sudden satisfaction. Suspicious and mean; points to bear in mind after civilized preliminaries. She had guessed that a middle-aged daughter so recently bereaved would be grateful for a new audience and she prepared to listen with understanding.

It was difficult, Betsey decided, to know which of them was enjoying it more.

"He always knocked on the wall when he was ready for me to get him up. Seven o'clock regular it always was. You could set a clock by him. This was on the Thursday. . . ."

Somewherc, Mrs. Thomas thought, her face set in sympathy, somewhere there must be a link, a link between this place and Greenwood and then with Victoria Varley. If the rest of the woman's cottage was like the room they were in now there could have been little to interest Greenwood. No, it must certainly have been what Gough had called "the old man's bits and pieces," but although she was convinced that Victoria Varley was somehow connected with Greenwood, that his visit there had not been purely coincidental, she could not think how that could have happened.

"Twenty past and not a sound. At first I thought, oh hullo, I thought, he's having a lic in. . . ."

Small and thin with scraped hair and an undernourished face, the broad Suffolk accent carefully upgraded as a concession to her visitors, she remembered every minute of the drama for them. She was, she told them, a Mrs. Teasdale and she had looked after her father since her mother had died. It seemed a long time ago and now they were both gone. Her own husband had been killed in the war.

"I called out to him, 'Dad!' I called, he never answered. He's gone, I thought. I knew it before I went upstairs. Twenty years younger he looked and not a line on his face."

"A terrible shock for you," Mrs. Thomas said with genuine kindness. "How old was he?"

"Ninety-two, but it never comes easy, does it?"

"No indeed, never easy."

"I took these on his ninetieth birthday."

The Polaroid snapshots she handed to Betsey showed the old man sitting proudly at his birthday tea-table, white-haired and straight. His room, Betsey thought, looked more cheerful than his daughter's. There was a fire in the grate, a row of Toby Jugs on the mantelshelf and some pictures on the wall behind him. For a moment one of them stirred a memory in the back of his mind but then it was gone.

"Your father liked paintings?" he asked, as he handed the little pile of snapshots to Mrs. Thomas.

"If you could call it painting, poor old chap, yes, he liked it."

"He painted himself?" Betsey asked.

"He came to it late, but it gave him something to do when he couldn't dig anymore. He used to copy anything, Christmas cards, advertisements in the colour mags. You wouldn't believe the mess he used to make in there. I was forever cleaning up. He had them stacked everywhere when he couldn't get any more on the walls. I couldn't scold him; he got like a child in the end,'' Mrs. Teasdale said, so overcome that she offered them a cup of tea.

''You never know when it's near,'' Mrs. Thomas said, watching the preparation of the tea with interest. One spoonful of tea for three didn't promise a stimulating brew. ''All that,'' she said encouragingly, ''and then the sale to cope with on top of everything.''

''What did you mean just now,'' Mrs. Teasdale said, swirling the teapot industriously at knee level, ''when you said, another one?'' She included Betsey in her question and he was grateful that Mrs. Thomas gave him no chance to show his embarrassing lack of information on the point.

''Estate agents,'' Mrs. Thomas said swiftly. ''They always get in first, don't they? All right, I suppose, for a quick sale. Still I mustn't grumble. Over and done with now. I never saw it advertised in his window. Sold to one of his rich clients on his waiting list, I suppose. Ah well.''

The word 'rich' seemed to galvanise Mrs. Teasdale. ''I haven't exchanged contracts yet! Sort of place you were looking for, was it?''

Mrs. Thomas nodded, safe in the knowledge that she had taken the trouble to find out exactly how much the cottage had fetched from the flat-chested young woman in Gough's front office. ''I might,'' she said, delicately draining her cup of tinted water, ''I might have gone quite high for it if I'd liked it.''

Mrs. Teasdale's age was uncertain. She was not a young woman but she could move remarkably quickly. Within fifteen minutes of taking the key of her father's cottage from its hook, she had shown them over it, the toy bedrooms, the kitchen and bathroom added to the living-room later, like her own. While the ladies were discussing plumbing and the height of the sink, Betsey, like dealers the world over, enjoyed himself assessing the old man's room. It was nothing special, some Victorian furniture, solid and dull.

The room was much as the old man had left it, a small museum to celebrate his life. His paintings covered the walls and had overflowed into stacked piles on the floor. ''Poor Dad's old daubs,'' his daughter had called them. Betsey found himself liking them more than she did. Flowers, stage coaches in deep snow, sleek modern cars sitting in the grandeur of Greek ruins. The old man had seen more than the things he had copied and given them a life they had never had as Christmas cards or advertisements in the Sunday supplements.

The Toby Jugs on the mantelshelf had far less appeal for him. One of his pottery books had compared them to elderly female traffic wardens, and since then he had never been able to look on them kindly. There was a mark in the dust where one of them had been taken away and a space on the wall above showing that the wallpaper had once been red and not faded pink. Someone had taken a painting, too.

He thought of the photographs and tried to remember what had caught his eye.

When they came in from the kitchen, Mrs. Teasdale came over and stood next to him.

''Mrs. Thomas tells me you own the antique shop in Flaxfield. You don't look like a dealer. I don't like dealers very much.''

''Mrs. Teasdale's had a rotten old time,'' Mrs. Thomas said soothingly, ''people coming to see the cottage.''

''Some of them didn't want the cottage at all, Nosy Parkers, just an excuse to poke around.'' Mrs. Teasdale looked at him accusingly.

He should have known better, he thought, than to offer Lizzie a lift. Doreen had warned him, but then Doreen was always warning him about her mother. And why was she standing bright-eyed and silent, ignoring his anguished looks for help?

"We're not all the same you know," he said. "I can assure you that is not the reason I'm here. My mother-in-law suffers from varicose veins. I offered to drive her, that's all. I promise you I don't want to buy anything here at all, absolutely nothing."

He was aware that he had not been very gentlemanly, but he felt cornered and unjustly accused.

"Dad thought a lot of his bits; he liked his Tobys." The look on her face was a curious mixture of suspicion and pleading. "Are they valuable?"

"I've never liked them very much, I'm afraid, but a lot of people do. These are not very old, late Victorian, not modern, so say about fifty pounds each? There're five of them. Yes, they ought to fetch at least two hundred and fifty pounds. I'll speak to Mr. Gough for you, if you like. He can put a reserve on them for you. Was that all he had? Just these five?"

"There was another," Mrs. Thomas said, joining them. "She sold it to the lady she cleans for once in a while. Now I think Mrs. Teasdale is wondering if perhaps she did the right thing. She doesn't like to ask her, you see."

Betsey sighed. He had been a dealer long enough to try and avoid situations like this. To comment on a deal already completed was a recipe for unpleasantness at best, and a screaming row if you were unlucky, with yourself in the middle of it and not a penny profit. If she had sold something of her own free will, then it was over and done with. He didn't like the look on Lizzie Thomas's face. She was far too pleased with herself.

"All the same," she said, "Mr. Trottwood will look at the snaps again for you before we go. Mrs. Teasdale used to work for Miss Varley."

She was already out of the door and moving happily down the garden path ahead of them before he could reply.

"Once it's all cleaned up, you could make that room lovely," Mrs. Teasdale said, catching up with them at the door of her own cottage. "Don't rush off. Let me freshen the pot for you."

The water she added was certainly fresh but it placed a severe strain on the already pathetic brew.

"You read about that poor Mr. Greenwood, of course?" Mrs. Thomas said. "Mr. Gough happened to mention he came to see next door."

"That wasn't the cottage he wanted," Mrs. Teasdale sniffed scornfully, "only to look at the furniture and things. I won't speak ill of the dead but I can't stand meanness. 'Silly Suffolk,' they say, but I didn't trust him. Twenty pounds he offered for all Dad's Toby Jugs! I wouldn't even let him see them. I told him straight, I got ten times that the day before for just one of them—well, that and one of his silly old paintings I wouldn't give houseroom to. Ugly old thing, mind you. That was only kindness on Miss Varley's part but I wasn't going to tell him that. Questions, questions. I was glad to see the back of him."

"But you mentioned Miss Varley's name to him?" Mrs. Thomas asked.

"Only her name. I never told him where she lived. I watched him go into the 'phone-box on the corner. He must have looked her up in the book. I haven't been up since, and she's never asked. I couldn't fancy it now. I couldn't even pass that lavatory let alone clean it, not after that, not knowing the man's face. I mean it's not like your own father, is it?"

"No, indeed. I never realised that you knew her. It's a small world, isn't it? What a terrible time you've had altogether. Nice, is she?"

"Miss Varley's all right on the right sort of day, as you might say. A bit free in her ways for some round here, but I speak as I find."

An amateur would have pursued an opening like that but Mrs. Thomas was not an amateur. Gossip, that casual exchange of unproven fact, was a pleasant pastime she had raised to the level of a fine art. Honed in the professional school of the Welsh valleys, in the unsophisticated flatlands of Suffolk she was like an Olympic gold-medallist unfairly competing at village sports. Mrs. Teasdale, for all her suspicious nature, had pronounced Miss Varley to be kind. If others were less well disposed towards her, then Mrs. Thomas knew that she would do well to cast her net among them.

"You've been very kind, Mrs. Teasdale. We wouldn't have bothered you if we'd known what you've been through," she said.

"No, it's been a change. I haven't seen many since Dad's cottage went."

"Dear old chap," Mrs. Thomas said, taking the photographs from Betsey. "You caught him a treat in these, I must say. Can you spare one? I think Mr. Trottwood would like to have one to make sure Mr. Gough knows what to look for when the sale comes up. We'll keep it safe for you. Ta."

There was no sense of ungainly haste in their leaving but Betsey was glad to find himself running down the garden path in the rain to start the car while Mrs. Thomas sheltered in the cottage doorway and said goodbye. He wasn't thinking about the Toby Jug but the painting in the photograph.

"When you say 'high,' " Mrs. Teasdale said, forced by their sudden departure into open ground, "how much would you have paid for Dad's place?"

Mrs. Thomas felt sorry for her. Like Churchill, she believed in magnanimity in victory. The woman was a money-grabber but there were worse faults than that. She took her arm kindly.

"It's not really quite right for me, my dear, but I hope you get every penny of fifteen thousand pounds." Since she knew that Mrs. Teasdale had verbally agreed to seventeen thousand pounds the relief on her face did not surprise Mrs. Thomas.

"Tell him to take care of the photograph," Mrs. Teasdale called after her visitor, as she ran through the rain to the car. "Those instant snaps are expensive!"

"Not a wasted journey," Mrs. Thomas said, as they drove back through the rain.

Betsey was very fond of Mrs. Thomas but he was also, he reminded himself, an antique dealer, and he wanted time to think. To think and to look at the photograph again.

"No," he said. "No, not wasted."

FIVE

The gallery of Fronefield and Greenwood Fine Arts in Kensington's prestigious Church Street was not as grand as their engraved business cards would suggest. It was not, strictly speaking, in the Church Street itself, but clung to its skirt around the corner in Pig Lane. There was a small flat over the gallery on the ground floor and a basement room which they had tried to cure of damp and failed.

Mrs. Thelma Fronefield sat at the desk in a corner of the gallery bulging anxiously out of her tailor-made and watching the preparations of her daughter Ruth with a mixture of pride and apprehension.

"A shop girl at my time of life. Imagine what the neighbours will say!"

"None of their business. You'll love it, Mummy, or I wouldn't have asked you. You always say that since Daddy died there's been nothing but bridge and television. I'm not taking much. I've got one more little case to bring down."

Mrs. Fronefield watched her daughter's high-heels disappear up the steep staircase and was glad she had brought some sensible shoes—not unsmart, thank God, but sensible.

"Anyway, it'll be a change for you," Ruth said, adding the case to the others she had packed, ready for the car and her journey to Suffolk, "and you know Auntie Rose will look after everything in Edgware for you."

"Into every drawer," Mrs. Fronefield said with deep family knowledge. "The washing machine going day and night and not a white sheet left in the house. Everything bright pink. My sister is not called Rose for nothing."

They were old jokes, told through the years with affection, so easy on the tongue that she could watch her daughter make coffee on a gas ring in the hearth without thinking of Rose at all but only of Ruth, with her sweet oval face and her father's eyes. Ruth still only a young woman and a widow already. Poor Joe, not the best choice, but who could tell children about marriage? And his heart had been in the right place, what there was of it. And Suffolk! What a place to die, if you could rely on television, bird sanctuaries full of choirs singing Benjamin Britten, and now trouble strong enough to drag Ruth from her home back to the scene of her husband's death. Hints, only hints for a mother who was ready to sacrifice her friends and her bridge and too proud to ask for concrete details. Thelma's face showed only intelligent concentration as Ruth went over the details of the running of the gallery yet again for her. It didn't seem possible that only yesterday Ruth was a schoolgirl brought up in a good humanist home with no religious nonsense, thank God.

"I'll let you know where I'm staying. I'm not sure yet. I may not be away long, anyway. It's just a question of someone holding the fort for a bit."

Mrs. Fronefield nodded sagely, vaguely seeing herself as a pioneer heroine loading John Wayne's rifles on a parapet.

"I've cleaned some drawers for you and a wardrobe, although why you had to bring all your fur coats I can't imagine."

"I think she must cook in them. Rose means well but she saves money on heating. It's a hobby. The Persian lamb still smells of fried fish from the last time."

She looked round the walls and wondered if Ruth and Joe had ever sold any paintings. She supposed they must have done, but although she had listened dutifully to her daughter talking knowledgeably about the Camden Town Group, the names of Gore and Gilman and Sickert meant nothing to her. She and Lionel had always liked the bright cheerful paintings they had bought in Harrods, where the sea could be purple but never the horses. Dear Lionel, she still missed his gentle wisdom: "It's fashion, Thelma, everything is fashion, colours come in and colours go out, it's no different from garments." Such tolerance; she would learn to love the dark muddy colours, and perhaps sell them all to a rich collector. There could be a commission possibly? And instantly she felt ashamed of herself. A widowed daughter with a real worry and dark rings under her eyes deserved respect and privacy, not a prying mother invading her dignity of silence with personal questions.

"This actress woman," she said, "was there anything between them?"

The question didn't annoy Ruth, she was only surprised that her mother had shown such reticence. It came as a relief.

"No, I don't think there was anything like that. It sounds cynical but he knew that sex might kill him. The specialist told us that. In the old days perhaps, before his heart, yes, he might have given some woman money then, he could be very generous, but not now, and Joe wasn't the sort to pay for a platonic friendship. He loved paintings not women."

In books, she had read of people's faces working. It would be unfair to leave her mother with her face working.

"No, nothing like that, Mummy. But, you see, Joe took rather a lot of money with him, and when he died—well, it wasn't with him; it was gone. I don't suppose I shall find out what happened or where it went to but I feel I've got to try."

"What do the police say?" Mrs. Fronefield was surprisingly calm.

"I can't tell the police. I can't have them asking questions. It was black money, that's what they call it. Joe didn't believe in paying income tax or V.A.T. if he could help it. If the tax people started to check the books I couldn't answer their questions, I'm sure of that. For all I know they could make me bankrupt. I'm sorry, Mummy, but that's how it is."

Mrs. Fronefield closed her eyes and shuddered. Well, it was no time for hysterics. A shock, but she would contain it; love and sympathy for a shock. Only the strength of the grip of her fingers on her daughter's arm betrayed the depth of her emotion.

"Find it or not, Ruth, you must repay money like that. No, listen! It's your father speaking, not only me. I'm not judging, Ruth! I can understand loyalty. Doubts? Yes, we had doubts about Joe for you. Did we speak against him?" Her fingers moved to her breast in a tight fist. "I stood with your father on the lawn of Buckingham Palace. We shook hands with the Queen of England and we never owed her a penny!

No, Ruth, a new life for you. You'll face it, like I did, with a clean conscience, if I have to give you every penny myself. How much was it?"

"About twenty thousand pounds, I think."

Mrs. Fronefield decided that only by washing up the coffee cups could she remain coherent. The staccato rattling of the cups in the saucers made her reconsider and she lowered them back to the desk with controlled slowness. When they were an inch above it she allowed them to crash dramatically.

"Do you want to kill me?"

It was a more natural and hopeful reaction, Ruth thought. Her mother was always easier to talk to once she'd taken the lid off.

It was much later when she eventually put her cases in the back of the Volvo and once more headed for the A 12 and Suffolk.

For a long time Thelma Fronefield sat at the desk, too full of thought to unpack or even to wash up. It was Lionel's fault; he should have been firmer with the girl, giving her everything she'd ever asked for. If Ruth hadn't taken the arts course at the auction house she wouldn't have met a crook like Joe. Even letting her use the family name for the gallery! It should be Greenwood and Greenwood the neighbours should read about if it ever got into the newspapers. It was a wonder the girl could keep so calm and determined. Well, that was something she'd got from her mother, at least. Twenty thousand pounds! And that wouldn't be the end of it all. There would be lawyers' fees and God knows what else to pay. Nobody could die without paying for it. Company taxes and everything valued that Joe had left, everything down to the last cup and saucer. She let her eyes wander over the paintings on the walls. That's what Ruth should do, get someone to value them for pennies not pounds. God knows it shouldn't be difficult with schlock like this. Taxes had been a terrible thing after Lionel, a daylight robbery. When the telephone rang she answered it without hesitation.

"Greenwood Gallery, can I help you?"

It was Mrs. Thomas's cat who first alerted her to the fact that Webber was wheezing. She wasn't deaf but Bunter had an acute sensitivity to the higher frequencies of incipient bronchitis. Every winter it had proved a useful indicator. She listened politely to Webber's account of his visit to Sarah Collins, their Flaxfield doctor, and, as usual, distrusted it.

"Basically true," Sarah Collins told her cheerfully. She had long ago decided that for purposes of medical etiquette she might just as well bracket them as husband and wife.

"Nothing serious. If we get some decent weather it will probably clear up. If not there's always antibiotics, but I don't like using them too soon. He ought to get away for a bit. Somewhere warm. It would help his arthritis, too. Why don't you go with him, Lizzie?"

"A break from me might do him as much good as the sunshine," Mrs. Thomas admitted honestly. "I push him a bit sometimes, you know. Anyway, I've got things to do."

"How are the legs?"

"I don't let them bother me."

"I expect we'll have to shoot you, in the end. Are you bidden to the vicarage rout next week?"

"I expect so, if Webber is fit enough."

It always amused Sarah Collins that she called him Webber to her friends and kept John for herself. For acquaintances or strangers she reserved Inspector Webber.

"We must make an effort, I think," said Sarah Collins. "I expect the vicar is about to launch an appeal for something or other. Poor Joan, she does hate dinner parties. Let's hope she doesn't attempt her suet pudding again. She's already been in for tranquillisers. She doesn't get them, of course, but she thinks she does and it seems to work.''

In the end Mrs. Thomas decided he had better go to Italy.

''It's no good reading the brochures, they're all full of lies, including the photographs. Tuscany should be warmer than France at this time of the year.''

He chose a small country hotel near Florence and waited to hear confirmation of his booking.

''Stick to pasta and don't touch any of their seafood and you'll be all right,'' she advised him, as they ate supper one night.

''Surely there won't be much fish so far inland?''

''Italians think mussels grow on trees. Keep it simple.''

He concentrated on his meal with gratitude and already regretted the Italian holiday. She was not always the most soothing of companions but her cooking, he reflected, was almost worth wheezing for. He wasn't going to press his luck, but it was strange that she seemed content to let him go off on his own. A suspicion that she might make a nuisance of herself while he was away crossed his mind and he dismissed it as unworthy. She seemed to have accepted that the unfortunate Mr. Greenwood had succumbed to natural causes. So that was over and done with; no mystery.

''I expect you'll find plenty to do while I'm away,'' he ventured, helping himself generously to more salad.

''I shall cootch quiet—like the lilies of the field.''

She was wearing a pinafore of turquoise and orange spots and he wondered if she remembered the end of her quotation. Yes, probably: ''Even Solomon in all his glory was not arrayed like one of these.'' He also wondered if the Villa Flavio would run to pretty waitresses.

''This is really very good, Lizzie. What is it?''

''Pressed pig's cheek. I've had it in brine for you.''

"It doesn't taste salty."

"You soak it," she said patiently, "and then cook it in dry cider with an onion and a couple of carrots. It's best cold like this with a few capers."

"I saw the television commercial you were telling me about last night," he said. "Victoria Varley weaning a husband from the pub with canned beer at home. Quite a smart-looking woman."

"She brought that Toby Jug into the shop yesterday. Wanted Betsey to value it for her, she said."

"And?"

"It's worth quite a lot apparently; more than she paid for it, anyway."

"I thought he disliked valuations."

"He seems to have changed his mind."

"And did she try and sell it to him?"

"No, she is going to give it back to Mrs. Teasdale; it wouldn't be fair to keep it, she thinks. She only wanted something to remember the old man by and she'd got one of his silly old paintings. She thought the Toby Jug didn't really belong to her; it would feel like stealing, she said. Finish the meat up; it doesn't keep well."

"Thank you, I will. It seems that Betsey and Doreen were wrong about her—what was it? 'Mean and a bit beady-eyed'? She sounds rather an honest woman to me."

"She is also having an affair with Harry Fellows."

"A bit young for her?"

"She doesn't try to hide it either; everyone seems to know about it."

"You've been asking around?"

"Yes, of course."

He wiped his plate clean with the last of his bread. "Yes, well, as I said, an honest woman."

SIX

Victoria Varley, Betsey thought, had definitely changed, and for the better. Or perhaps he and Doreen had misjudged her. First the warm welcome when he had arrived, when she had greeted him like an old friend, and now, with his valuation almost completed, she made a pot of tea and sat drinking it with him. On the odd occasions when she had come into the shop, she had been dressed conventionally in thc uniform of the Home Counties: a coat and skirt with a blouse, although she had never worn a hat. She was obviously proud of her fair hair, which had been expensively cut and dyed. Now, out of uniform, it tumbled attractively over the shoulders of a check shirt. The tailored skirt of blue denim could only have been worn, he thought, by someone with her slim figure. The face was still good, but with a careful attention to detail of make-up that a younger woman needn't have bothered about, the top lip painted to make it full and the stain of shadow on the eyelids, which only drew attention to the lines at the corners of her eyes.

"What made you change your mind?" she said.

"About the valuation?" He sipped his tea and considered. Tell her that he wanted a closer look at the painting he'd seen only in a poor photograph? No, not for the moment anyway. "To be honest," he said, "I thought it was good of you to want to return the Toby Jug. People aren't always as nice as that. She must have been delighted."

"I'm afraid Mrs. Teasdale is not a very nice woman; she used to steal tea and washing powder."

"She still doesn't make a good cup of tea," he said.

"I suppose she used to look on it as perks and not stealing. She probably thought that I wouldn't miss things and that, anyway, I could afford it. Her way of justifying herself."

"People do that."

"She has a very poor opinion of antique dealers, by the way."

Betsey sighed. "I went to see the old man's cottage with my mother-in-law. I expect she told you that I thought his Tobys were worth about fifty pounds each? Well, so they are. I didn't see the one she sold to you, only in a snapshot, and you can't tell from that. If I'd seen it properly I'd have told her what I told you yesterday."

Victoria nodded. "That's why I took it back to her. I wasn't going to have her telling everyone that I'd robbed her of an heirloom. Things like that have a way of getting about. I'm sure you must have found that, too?"

He wanted to ask her about Greenwood and what it felt like to discover a dead man sitting on your lavatory. That would be too blunt, he thought, and he was afraid of changing the pleasant atmosphere. And then there was the painting; he dearly wanted to examine it closely. Don't push, he told himself.

"I could ask you the same thing, you know. Why did you change your mind about having your things valued?"

"Sheer vanity. I hadn't realised that your memory was so good. It's very flattering to be remembered."

He remembered her very well, a pretty, even a beautiful girl playing, sometimes, quite good parts.

"So what went wrong?" She smiled at him and at his

unspoken question. "Darling, if I knew that I wouldn't be advertising tins of disgusting beer, would I?"

This was better, she thought. The less the subject of that wretched Teasdale was discussed, the safer she felt. If people were going to talk, let them talk about things that didn't matter, things they knew about already. He seemed an amiable enough creature, this man Trottwood, with his ridiculous ill-fitting wig and his solemn, pussycat face. It was a type she knew well from her life in the theatre and the studios. Gentle and kind with a sense of humour, she remembered them as dressers or designers.

It was hard to resist such a good listener and over tea she told him her life story, because she couldn't resist the way his eyes widened with genuine interest. As a barmaid, Bessie Pipe had gone from Lambeth to become a night-club hostess in Soho and, after marrying a drunken television producer, had become Victoria Varley.

"I don't think his death had anything to do with it when the parts stopped coming. He did have some influence, of course. Contacts. We met people. No, it wasn't that, although I used to pretend it was at the time. Well, I would, wouldn't I? I felt sorry for him, too, in a way. A rotten life and a rotten. . . . Anyway, I got this house. It's rent-controlled and cheap enough, and I kissed his sister at his funeral which says something for me I suppose. Actually she was the one who got me into the commercials; she worked for an advertising agency."

Victoria in full flood was difficult to stop, and, in any case, he was too interested to try. The painting he so much wanted to see was propped against the wall in a dark corner of the room, but unfortunately behind him and out of his line of sight, and he was determined to let it rest until he could examine it properly. He believed in patience. It was getting late and the light was fading. It would be better to see it in daylight. It occurred to him that it was more important to consolidate his new-found friendship. He could come back and finish the valuation another day. The poor light, which he could use as an excuse, flattered her. In daylight the skin at the neck of the check shirt had looked like a plucked chicken. Now, in the softer light from the log fire, she looked remarkably like the girl he remembered. That's what was wrong, he thought. She should have abandoned the imitation of youth. There were plenty of young actresses without chicken skin and crow's feet. Perhaps, with scraped-back hair, glasses, and thin lips, she could be working yet. He didn't tell her that, instead he astonished her by remembering exactly the clothes she had worn in every episode of an old television series called "The Passing Show," and confiding that he had himself once danced, as a child, in pantomime.

When Harry Fellows let himself in with his own key he nodded amiably to Betsey to show that they knew each other and sat, in his working clothes, in an armchair near the fire. In the poor light it was difficult to tell whether his silence was polite or whether he resented finding someone talking and laughing with Victoria. His "goodnight" to Betsey as she showed him to the door seemed courteous enough but non-committal. A very attractive young man.

Harry knew he was attractive and he had learned that people liked you even more if you pretended not to know it. Women especially; they liked it if you pretended to be shy. A bit shy and a bit rough. They liked that, even when they were quite famous and appeared on television. They let you sit by their fire and paid for you in the pub, making you take the money before you went in. Sometimes you had to fuck her but it wasn't too bad and not too often. She didn't like him using that word, not even if he said it shyly. That was funny for an actress. You had to talk about going to bed and then you could fuck her silly.

She wasn't silly though, not about money, she wasn't.

Betsey told her not to walk out to the car with him but the chill evening air didn't seem to worry her.

"It won't last, of course," she said almost casually. "At first I thought it was only sex but I've done that stupid thing and fallen in love with him. I've tried the tinned beer trick but the commercial boys seem to have got it wrong again. I thought I'd had enough of pubs when I was behind the bar, but if that's what he likes, then so do I. He likes people to see us together. That's sweet, isn't it? He doesn't like me to call him a baby but that's what he is, which makes me a cradle-snatcher, I suppose— No, I don't suppose at all. It doesn't matter. I can't do anything about it, even if I wanted to. It's something that's never happened to me before. Does that sound ridiculous?"

"No," he said truthfully. "No, it doesn't."

When they got to the car she hugged herself against the chill of the deserted lane. "Will you come again? It's my fault that you couldn't finish; I talk too much."

"Yes, of course, I'd like to. There's only the sitting-room left, anyway." The sitting-room and the painting, he thought.

"I often have to go up to London to see my agent. I'll ring you."

He nodded and then beamed with relief as he succeeded in coaxing the engine into reluctant life.

"Run along in," he said maternally. "You'll catch your death."

In the days that followed, Flaxfield had its first false summer. It was something that the natives of Suffolk expected. Suddenly, there would be warm sunshine almost before the snow had gone, and people would blossom and say it looked as though they would miss spring altogether again. Ruth Greenwood, after some considerable difficulty, had persuaded Mr.

Gough to rent her a cottage. There were conditions, he explained to her, but perhaps if he used his good offices with the vicar, they need not be insurmountable. The cottage was church property.

"I would pay rent in advance, of course."

"I shall speak to Mr. Coley," Gough said executively.

In the warm sunshine under a sky of cloudless blue, Webber's wheezing improved dramatically and he complained that the holiday was unnecessary. Flaxfield was his home, he said stubbornly, and his garden could not be deserted at a time when it most needed him. Mrs. Thomas would have none of it. Every winter, she pointed out, his bronchitis and his arthritis got worse and she had no intention of ignoring Dr. Collins's advice. In the end he felt it was easier to admit defeat and he resigned himself to her preparations, only putting his foot down when she seemed about to order a mosquito net. The travel company confirmed his booking and it was agreed that he would fly from Gatwick in a few days' time.

It was not to be.

William Coley sat at his desk searching for an inspiration for Sunday's sermon, while his wife struggled dutifully to make some sense of an unsuitable mixture of clashing flowers in a vase which was refusing to accommodate them with elegance. Only Joan, he thought ruefully, could contrive to make such an appalling noise with a pair of scissors. It was her way, he knew, of indicating politely that she wanted to talk to him, for she usually arranged his flowers silently in the kitchen.

"Very nice," he said, looking approvingly at the curious offering and ignoring the chaos of stalks and leaves on the carpet.

She gave the vase a final shake and abandoned it with

resignation. "Perhaps they'll settle," she said, although she didn't believe they would. "What I don't understand, William, is how she knew that the cottage was in your gift anyway."

"Church property? She spoke to Mr. Gough about finding somewhere to live, only temporarily, I'm afraid. But it's better than leaving it empty, I feel. Apparently, she quite took a fancy to the village when she came down for the inquest. She feels near him here, she tells me. I can understand that, poor woman."

"But surely the cottage is meant to be used for the church caretaker? She doesn't seem the sort of woman who would want to be a caretaker, William."

"So Mr. Gough explained to her, but she seems quite happy with the arrangement. The caretaker duties are hardly arduous, after all. I more or less invented the position as a sinecure, you remember, and since there are no parishioners in dire need at the moment, Mrs. Greenwood is welcome to it until a more permanent incumbent appears."

Joan was on her knees collecting leaves so that she didn't have to look directly at him as she said, "William, you know I never interfere, but has it occurred to you that Mrs. Greenwood might be Jewish?"

"No, I don't think it has. Is she? Yes, I suppose she could be. She is certainly very striking, as was indeed her namesake in the Old Testament. She too was down on her luck, of course, and far from home. Keats put it rather well I always think: 'She stood in tears amid the alien corn.' I hope Mrs. Greenwood won't be homesick among us. I think not," he added cheerfully, ignoring the doubt on his wife's face. "I don't think her religion would preclude her in any way. The last caretaker I seem to remember was a Methodist."

There wasn't any point in pursuing it, she thought. Perhaps he was right, although she thought that sometimes William carried Christianity too far.

He had turned to his desk and started writing again. Perhaps the story of Ruth had kindled an idea for a sermon. She hoped not. In the Bible, Ruth had always seemed to her to be a particularly pushy woman and probably no better than she should be. She had certainly done very well for herself among strangers.

Joan stood holding her apron full of leaves and flower stalks, looking over William's head of thinning hair to a quiet corner of the churchyard where Harry Fellows had hung his shirt over a tombstone and was scything the long grass between the graves. It must be Wednesday, then. Harry only came on Wednesdays and Fridays, unless there was extra work for him to do. A temporary caretaker and a part-time sexton, how pleasant it would be if Flaxfield were a rich living and they could afford to employ people full time, instead of this miserable scrimping and saving and William's never-ending appeals for money. What a really beautiful young man he was, with his sulky mouth and his laughing eyes and the shock of his brown arms and neck against the white of his strong body. Difficult to tell his age. Twenty-five? Thirty? No good asking William; he would never discuss Harry. A full-time sexton, of course, might be old and flabby. She supposed it must be true that he was Victoria Varley's lover; everyone said they made no secret of it. She wondered if they had sex every night and if she made him bath first. Perhaps she liked the smell of sweat and grass cuttings. William had asked her to the dinner party, but it was hardly a question you could ask someone you scarcely knew over coffee.

"What is she like?" she had asked William, when he had thought of inviting her.

"I liked her. The sort of woman who knows her own mind."

In the sitting-room of Fox House, Betsey stood in front of the painting with Victoria and saw it clearly for the first time. The sun that shone down on Harry Fellows lit up every corner of it with the colours bright and clear.

"Are you quite sure?" he said.

"Quite sure. I made up my mind before you came."

SEVEN

Benjamin Lamb didn't expect to beat April when they played tennis. It was simply that it seemed a good idea while he was waiting, as patiently as he could, to hear from Joseph Greenwood. It gave them something to occupy their minds and he felt that the rich food at the Norland was probably reducing her efficiency as a strong-arm companion. It made sense, like taking a dog for a walk. The head porter at the Norland who, for the right kind of money could get tickets for anything, had found a private court for them in York House Square. At match point he watched her prance to receive his serve, her Norland-fed breasts bouncing impressively, like melons in slow motion. They didn't seem to get in her way as she returned the ball straight at his body with the speed of a space rocket. In self-defence, he held his racquet in front of him with both hands on the frame and contrived a lucky drop shot. She killed it with a low vicious backhand which he acknowledged with a shudder of recognition and approval.

They changed and showered in the primitive wooden pavilion which reminded him of prison. It depressed April, too.

"My God, Ben, this place stinks." When he was silent she said, "You wanna talk about it?"

That was one of the reasons she was hooked on him. He would talk if you asked him. American men didn't talk to you, they talked at you, about themselves. She didn't love him, she thought, but she was hooked on him. Ben was different, even here in his own country, where his accent was the same as all the others. Ben was really something.

They stowed their tennis gear in the car he'd rented and ate sandwiches in a pub only marginally cleaner than the changing-room. It didn't inhibit her appetite and every one of her teeth registered on the bread and the cheese like a horseshoe.

"I can't go—I don't want to go—until I've seen Joe," he said at last. "If he says he's on to something big then we'll stay."

"He's good?"

"Meaning he knows his job? Yes."

"So where is he?"

"I don't know. When he cancelled the meal he was on his way to see something. He said he'd be in touch."

She licked her fingers and attacked another sandwich. "You wanna tell me?"

"Does the name Spencer mean anything to you?"

"Sure. Lady Diana. She married someone, I watched it on TV."

"Stanley Spencer. A painter—an English painter. Modern. He died about 1960. I believe he's the best we've ever had, and I'm including Blake and Hogarth. Joe thought he'd found one.''

''You don't want your sandwich? Found one where?''

''He could have been 'phoning from anywhere in England.''

''You said he has a gallery, so why don't we ask?''

''Joe works in his own way; he may not have told them anything. Some deals can be very delicate. You should know that.''

''He could have sold it to someone else.''

''Perhaps. I hope not.'' He made it sound like a threat. ''He likes cash. I pay cash and no receipts. I don't want to mess anything up.''

She finished the crumbs on her plate, pinching them into scraps of putty with bits of cheese, and marvelled at his restraint. ''There's no chance he could have phoned the hotel and they forgot to tell you?''

''Not the Norland; they know I'm waiting.''

The words ''he could have sold it to someone else'' stuck in his head like a cracked record. It made him feel sick. He remembered first seeing some illustrations of Spencer's paintings in a book in the prison library, and that night he had cried in his cell, because he knew that Stanley Spencer had understood pain and loneliness and love. That was why Benjamin reckoned he could find plenty of rich Americans who would pay a million for him. Pounds, not dollars. Americans wanted the best of everything and they didn't mind paying for it.

Even before she spoke, Thelma Fronefield knew that the woman was American. April couldn't have been anything else. She warmed when the man introduced himself as Dr. Lamb in an English accent and said he was an old friend of her son-in-law. It had been a long time since she had had the luxury of comforting someone other than her close family. Not since the war and the bombing. She locked the door swiftly and arranged chairs for them to sit and enjoy the shock in comfort. She would have given them hot, sweet tea, but you made tea and you lost eye contact. In air-raid shelters there had always been an urn full of it; you only had to turn the tap.

"Heart," she murmured. "A massive coronary, they said at the inquest. They found him on . . . on a Thursday," she amended tactfully—a man deserved dignity in death, even Joseph. "A shock for us all, as you can imagine."

Benjamin could imagine; he was grateful for the chair.

"My daughter has gone down to Suffolk again—to sort out his business affairs. That is why she turned to me. Where else would a daughter turn, with a husband cremated already?"

His suit was good, she noted. Quality cloth and the lapels handstitched. He had better taste than his American wife. Perhaps they were staying in London for a while. A good hotel. They might play bridge, they might have a friend who would make a fourth. It would comfort them more than sweet tea. She could wear the mink. Poor man, he looked shattered.

Benjamin rallied. Suffolk: well, that was something. That stupid cow April. Why hadn't she spoken earlier? God knows what was happening in bloody Suffolk. Even in distress, his eyes assessed the pictures on the walls of the gallery. Thelma Fronefield would have been delighted to know that his opinion was a more informed version of her own. Poor pickings—second-rate Duncan Grant; London Group. The Gertler wasn't bad, but no front runners, not like . . . another thought struck him like iced water on his stomach. Suppose Greenwood had somehow got the painting back to London? Perhaps his wife— What the hell was her name? Perhaps she already had it hidden away somewhere here in the gallery. The mother, thank God, was a compulsive talker. He already had Suffolk; let her talk. He wished he could remember the name of Joseph Greenwood's wife.

Thelma was gratified at the effect of her news and couldn't resist the warmth of his sympathy. In the time she had been in charge of the gallery, she had encountered quite a number of American women, but very few had she been able to stun into shocked silence. The man was even more of a puzzle—a doctor, yet a business acquaintance, and an old friend. Who better to confide in? Not her private opinion of Joseph, of course, and not the missing money. For a friend that would be unkind. The drama of the death and the inquest she could not deny herself. She even abandoned Joseph's dignity and told them about the lavatory. Who else but a doctor should understand such intimate details? Benjamin nodded sympathetically and recovered enough to adjust his approach.

"Poor man, I knew he had a heart problem. We were only business friends, of course. I have not practised medicine for many years. The world of art has been my whole life."

"The pull of the paint! I should know. Ruth could have walked wholesale into her father's fashion business—contacts in Hong Kong and the Queen's Award for Industry—but no, she knew what she wanted and we encouraged her. Do you and Mrs. Lamb play bridge, Doctor?"

"Sadly, no. In fact we are moving on quite soon. We're at the Norland at present. Strangely enough Suffolk is our next destination. I must try and see Ruth. I might be of some practical help to the poor girl. It is the least I can do. Do you know exactly where I can contact her?"

Chantry Cottage suited Ruth well enough, although it had been empty for so long that the dirt and neglect was depressing at first sight. She had been glad of something to occupy her mind. It was all very well simply installing yourself in a village four miles away from where Joe had died, but she had no idea what she should do next. She could hardly knock on Victoria Varley's door and say, "Excuse me, I couldn't bring myself to speak to you after the inquest but my husband died on your lavatory and there seems to be rather a lot of money missing." Something had happened and she was going to find out what it was. She was only mildly shocked to realise that it was the money, even more than Joe's death, that obsessed her.

It was curious to be in the midst of a community and yet not of it. She felt like the women on television who went to live in hostile African villages. The cottage wasn't much better than their grass huts, either. She remembered that it was considered the correct thing not to push yourself forward. Sooner or later curiosity would overcome them and some of the natives would approach shyly. In fact it had already begun. There was a nice young man called Harry Fellows and a friendly little woman who wasn't stand-offish like the others. She had already offered to come and help her clean up the cottage. A Mrs. Thomas. It was remarkably lucky to find someone so easy to talk to, someone who seemed to enjoy even the most exhausting household chores and obviously tackled them purely in the spirit of good neighbourliness. It had been a long time since Ruth had laughed so happily or talked so freely.

On the morning of the vicarage dinner party, Webber went to see Sarah Collins at the surgery. He was the last patient in the waiting-room and after her examination he buttoned his shirt while she made coffee in cracked and definitely unhygienic cups.

"Very good. Well done, John. Practically back to normal—well, let's say normal for East Anglia. Anyway, your chest is quite clear and you seem to be holding your own with the arthritis."

"It doesn't bother me."

"Quite right."

"I'll reckon it time to worry when I join the stick and crutch brigade. The sun clears it up."

"You'll be getting plenty of that soon, lucky old devil. Looking forward to it?"

"No. Lizzie's idea. She panics. It's easier to give in."

"How is she?"

"I haven't seen much of her lately. I suspect she's keeping out of my way, playing the Good Samaritan with the Greenwood woman."

"I've seen them around; they seem very thick together. This coffee is disgusting, isn't it?"

"A bit soapy, but it's wet and warm. I know she has to wear those elastic stockings, but can't you persuade her to use a calmer colour? Her legs look as though she boils them in beetroot."

"She could choose any shade she wants. She's got very definite ideas about colour. I'm only her doctor, not her dressmaker." It was bad enough, she thought, trying to sort out the marital problems of her patients when they were really married. "You could suggest she wears a long dress for the vicar's do tonight. I suppose you're both going?"

"Yes. I'll try, if I see her before I collect her. I mustn't sit gossiping—I've got my housework to do these days."

Betsey came into the vicarage kitchen beaming with gentle reassurance. Joan Coley had wisely confined her tears to the afternoon, when he had helped her with the final alterations to her dress. Poor Joan, not even the pick of the jumble sales, he thought. Only the leftovers her conscience allowed her to claim when the sales had finished.

"What do you think?" she asked miserably.

"Turn around. Well, anyone can see it's not a Paris model, dear, but then it never was. Never mind, it's a good material and the colour suits you— Do you feel safe with the straps?"

"I think so, if I don't try anything sudden. I suppose I could have asked William for some extra housekeeping and then perhaps I could have found something in Ipswich. Just a simple dinner dress, nothing grand."

He gave her a brotherly kiss on her overpowdered cheek, reeking of Californian Poppy. He could easily have bought her a dozen dresses but knew better than even to hint at such a breach of etiquette. As a vicar's wife she was allowed to dispense charity but not to receive it. In any case her faith in Ipswich as a reliable source of simple dinner dresses was misplaced. Almost everything about Joan, he thought sadly, was misplaced, except her touching love for her husband.

"Thank you, dear. I do hate it all, only William is so very keen on duty. Have they all arrived yet or have I got time for a quick oven-check?'

"Everyone except Victoria Varley. I've taken the sherry round again, so they're quite happy. Check away. What are you giving us?" he asked brightly. Joan's culinary skill seldom ventured beyond salads and sandwiches. "Anchovies do I smell?"

"It does have anchovies in it. How clever of you. I felt it would cheer it up a bit. It's a sort of farewell tribute for John Webber's Italian holiday. I got it from one of the old church magazines. Pilchard and spaghetti roast. Do tell me if you think it's brown enough on top. I've stupidly lost one of my contact lenses so I've taken the other one out, too. I would have had a joint, only meat is so expensive and William is such a generous carver, I couldn't bear it not to go round like the last time. You are a comfort. That should be big enough even for seconds, don't you think?"

"Quite brown enough," he said, closing the oven door firmly, "and more than enough for everyone. I'll put these tins in the dustbin and then we really must go in." The tins were labelled "Pilchards in Tomato Sauce," and bore the legend "Reduced: Special Offer—33 pence only."

Betsey gallantly offered her his arm, as much for his own support as hers. It was not the moment, he felt, to discuss recipes. She smiled at him with myopic gratitude.

"Right, Joan dear, chin up, straight back, and quick march."

Victoria Varley, for reasons best known to herself, did not appear, and at nine o'clock, when the sherry ran out, it was decided to eat without her. The dinner was no more disastrous than usual. Coley talked earnestly and at great length about the restoration fund for the church tower, which helped to divert attention from the monstrous meal. Only Doreen committed herself to a second helping in a desperate effort to change the subject. Charity did not come easily to Doreen. She was not a giver and she fought a gallant evasive action throughout the treacle sponge and the flaky-pastry cheese fingers. She was well aware that Betsey would give something, probably without telling her, but she had enjoyed the skirmish.

At half-past ten Betsey made coffee with Joan in the kitchen and prepared to help her carry it in.

Their entrance was delayed by a knock at the kitchen door, which opened on to the vicarage garden. Betsey opened it to reveal a worried-looking Harry Fellows.

"I'm very sorry, Mrs. Coley, and I won't keep you. I don't want to speak to her because I know you've got guests an' all, but I just wanted to know if Miss Varley turned up all right?"

EIGHT

The next morning Betsey got up early and looked long and critically at the painting he had bought from Victoria Varley. It was a view of a sea shore, such as might have been seen from a promenade, looking down over some beach huts, across the shingle and out to the open sea, where a funnelled ship sat on the water like a child's toy. At the edge of the sea, two fishermen in oilskins were hauling their nets from boats pulled up on the beach, a cascade of shining fish spilling out over their feet. They were looking at a third man, pointing an outstretched arm at them, who seemed to be telling them what to do. Perhaps he was a foreman of some sort, because he was wearing a Norfolk jacket with a bowler hat of authority above his glaring eyes. In tiny, childish letters on the bottom of the canvas the painting was titled "The *S.S. Mativig*," and in the corner in the same minuscule script, Mrs. Teasdale's father had proudly signed his name: Abner Gosse. Not a name, he thought sadly, to ruffle a sale-room or bring joy to the hearts of the ring.

When at last he had been able to look at it properly in Victoria's house, his first reaction had been one of bitter disappointment and he had laughed at the secret dream he had kept to himself. The dream every dealer has, that one day he will discover a hidden masterpiece and a fortune. He looked at it again sadly. It was certainly in the style of Stanley

Spencer, no one could deny that, but a Spencer as it might have been copied by a pavement artist. He had valued it for her at only a hundred pounds, more for politeness' sake than anything else. A crude daub by a senile old man who had probably copied it from a postcard or an illustration in a magazine. She would be lucky to get a hundred pounds for it. When she had seemed disappointed and told him that she had read in the newspapers that primitive paintings had been fetching quite good prices in the sale-rooms recently, he had obligingly agreed that perhaps three hundred pounds would be nearer the mark. When she had then offered to sell it to him for that sum, he had surprised himself by accepting. Crude though it was, the subject of the painting was intriguing and, like so many of the things he had accumulated through the years, he had bought it on impulse. When he had first seen it in the Polaroid photograph hanging over the old man's fireplace, it had made his heart thud with excitement. Here, in the hard light of the early morning, the reality was sad and without magic.

It was early. Doreen was still asleep. He turned and viewed the empty street.

In Flaxfield, as in most villages, the pub and the church were the main centres of social gathering. Trottwood Antiques had an advantage over them in that its opening hours were not restricted. Betsey himself combined some of the functions of both priest and publican and his shop was more comfortable than either The Bull or St. Peter's. The High Street was no longer empty. In the distance and from opposite directions, Mrs. Thomas and John Webber could be seen advancing towards each other. It was almost time to take Doreen her early morning tea and hot lemon juice, but he settled his wig and waited eagerly for company.

Neither of them would hurry, he thought. They would adjust their pace so that they would meet conveniently outside his shop, where, he had no doubt, they had both decided to come. It reminded him irresistibly of the scene in *High Noon*—nearly everything reminded Betsey of the films of his youth—the empty street and their two lonely figures. He watched Webber straighten his back as if to reassure her that his morning stiffness had disappeared with the early sunshine, and he noted with interest the colour of his mother-in-law's felt hat. For many years she had favoured the model worn by Celia Johnson in *Brief Encounter*, and it came in many different shades. The colour was often an indication of her mood and today she had chosen a submissive tone of donkey brown. There would be no shoot-out this morning, he felt. A decision had been taken. He watched them meet and talk, saw Webber's arm slip protectively round the shoulders of her ungainly trench coat and lead her towards the shop.

"I'm making tea for Doreen," Betsey said, when they had settled themselves. "She's lying in a bit. I don't think Joan's dinner agreed with her. I'll make some for all of us."

"John is not going to Italy," Mrs. Thomas said, with what Betsey thought was remarkable composure. Indeed, she spoke with every sign of positive relief.

"You mustn't judge Italian cooking by Joan's spaghetti. She means well. Italian pasta is quite different," Betsey told him.

"Thank you, tea would be very welcome," Webber said. "Tell me, what else did young Fellows say when you saw him last night?"

"Not much. He was hoping she'd be there, that's all. He was worried because he hadn't seen her for a day or so. She has a flat in London and I told him that I thought he might reach her there, but he said he didn't have the phone number, only the address somewhere in Chelsea. She told me that she sometimes goes up to see her agent. She's probably been caught up with business; theatrical agents can be very time-wasting. That seemed to reassure him."

Mrs. Thomas sat and watched them talking, but said nothing.

"There's quite a difference in their ages," Webber said. "Perhaps she's giving him a gentle hint, trying to shake him off?"

"No, I don't think so. She told me she was in love with him."

"And Fellows?"

"I don't know. He sleeps with her, of course. He likes people to see them together. He takes her out to pubs, she said. I like him. A bit shy, but a nice lad." He caught Mrs. Thomas's eye but she returned his look blankly and said nothing. It was something more than Joan's pasta, he thought. Somehow, at high noon, she had turned John into a policeman again and probably she had intended to all along.

"Is that the painting you bought from her?" Webber asked.

"Yes."

"Is it as good as you thought—from the photograph?"

"No, it's something the old man painted himself. I was wrong."

"What made you buy it?"

"I don't know. I couldn't resist it. It's not like any of his other stuff, and yet it is, in a way. When I saw it in the Polaroid, I thought it was by a man called Stanley Spencer, and I got excited. I wanted it, if I could. Greed, John. Once a dealer, always greedy. Even nice old Betsey. We get very near to the jungle sometimes."

"If you'd thought it was a genuine Spencer I'm sure you'd have paid her more for it," Webber said soothingly.

Betsey considered. Somehow it was a change to be able to shock Webber. "I expect I would. Yes, I would, but nothing like what it was worth. I'd probably have persuaded myself that I was taking a gamble. Anyway, I couldn't have afforded what it was really worth.''

Webber looked at him with interest. Betsey as a jungle predator was something new.

Doreen had grown tired of waiting. She appeared in the doorway in a dressing-gown and sipping hot lemon. ''My God, I need this after that ghastly food. I wonder I wasn't up half the night.''

Nobody answered her and she sat and sipped.

''And if it had been genuine,'' Webber said, ''how much would it have been worth?''

''Stanley Spencer?'' Betsey considered. ''God knows, I can't remember the last time he came up at auction. I don't think you could put a price on him now. It would depend on the subject, too. He painted a few pot boilers in his time, but for his real work? Twenty thousand pounds? Perhaps twenty times as much as that.'' He looked at the old man's painting sadly. ''What a pity. Half close your eyes in a bad light and you could be looking at a fortune.''

''But it's a copy?''

''Yes, a bloody poor one, too.''

''But you still bought it.''

''I told you—I couldn't resist it.''

There was a silence between them which Doreen, after appraising her mother's face, decided not to break, and she went to the kitchen to make her own tea.

For a while Webber sat looking at the painting, then rose and nodded pleasantly to Betsey.

''Still busy with Mrs. Greenwood?'' he asked Mrs. Thomas.

''She's pretty well straight, now. Perhaps we could have a meal about seven? If that suits you.''

''It will suit very well, thank you.''

When he'd gone, she turned and watched him walk down

the street, where a few early shoppers and cars were dressing the film set. When she looked back at Betsey she winked without smiling but remained silent. He wasn't temperamentally equipped to cope with silence, especially from Mrs. Thomas. It made him nervous and liable to drop things or to blurt out the first thing that came into his head, like "Are you going to marry John one day?" Or "Doreen wonders if you've ever slept with him."

He settled for "What did you say to make him change his mind?"

"Ruth Greenwood says that her husband had twenty thousand pounds in notes on him when he left home. It disappeared."

"He could have spent it somewhere else."

"He could. John doesn't think so. Neither do I. What was so special about this man Stanley Spencer?"

"There was a big exhibition at the Royal Academy," Doreen said. "Tea, Mam? It is fresh; I've just made it. We queued up for hours. I didn't think it would be worth it, but it was. They brought them from all over the world. It was wonderful."

Mrs. Thomas looked at her daughter with interest. You learned something new every day. She had never thought of Doreen as an art lover. Even allowing for Betsey's enthusiasm, which could account for her queuing for hours, it was unlike Doreen to consider it not only worth the effort but to describe the result as wonderful. It would be useless asking her why.

"What made it wonderful?" she asked Betsey.

He lifted his arms helplessly. "I could talk for hours but never get near it." He ran his fingers carefully through his wig in a gesture of controlled excitement. From a bookshelf in the corner of the shop he produced a thick catalogue of the Spencer exhibition, the thin cover protected with brown paper. "It's all in here. He was a funny little monkey of a man and a genius. He was born in a small village. Cookham, in Berkshire. He practically never left it all his life except for wars and a few other times. Cookham was his whole life and his religion, if you like. He painted everything just as though it had happened there in the village. The Resurrection was in Cookham churchyard and the Crucifixion he put in Cookham High Street. He painted other things, too—fat women and love and trees and flowers and his wives and his children. They aren't paintings at all, but real people. He saw Christ in a straw hat, preaching from a punt at Cookham Regatta. 'Poor old Jesus,' he used to call him and he talked about him and the Apostles as 'J.C. and Co.' 'I can see them very clearly,' he told someone, 'like a photograph of a football team with their arms folded and looking tough.' He was great, really great. I love him."

In that moment, Doreen loved her husband again, too. They didn't always get along very well, but she saw him now as Spencer might have seen him, like Christ himself, red and sweating, with a crooked wig and trying to convert her mother, a fat dumpy woman in a trench coat wearing elastic stockings and filled with doubt.

Mrs. Thomas doubted less than Doreen thought. "Can I borrow this catalogue? I promise I'll take care of it."

Betsey hesitated and then nodded.

"I hope you will, Mam. We can't get another, you know. They're like gold," Doreen said.

"Ta, love. I'll watch it." Cheeky little madam, but the wrong time to make a fuss. She could always slap Doreen down later if necessary.

At the door, she handed Betsey a folded scrap of paper. "I found this in the fish pie last night. I didn't like to say anything at table. It's Joan's contact lens. I thought it was too big for a pilchard scale so haven't chewed it. You can say you found it somewhere.''

Webber took a long, deep breath without a sign of a wheeze. The early spring sunshine was more than a passing promise, it was truly warm and he was walking well, in a street where he could buy English tobacco and the fish-and-chip shop was receiving a morning delivery of plaice and cod that had been swimming in the North Sea less than six hours ago. He considered Ruth Greenwood, the empty Varley house at Wangford, and Harry Fellows. There was a lot to think about.

He walked briskly to the outskirts of the village where the hideous new housing estate huddled under sufferance. The police station looked like all its boxlike neighbours, distinguished only by the notice board in the garden, with its warnings of Colorado beetles and bicycle thieves. With luck he would catch Sergeant Burnstead before he left.

He was given the respect due to his old rank and shown into the sitting-room while the children shouted in the kitchen and were shushed by the sergeant's mousey wife. Burnstead was so startlingly fair that he was almost albino. He had the broad Suffolk speech that Webber himself had been forced to modify when he was younger. Webber liked him and Burnstead talked to him easily.

''No, not what you'd call a formal report, Mr. Webber, no more'n chatting, like. I know Harry well. Sometimes in The Bull and sometimes over to Wangford in The Poacher's Arms—we're on the same darts team there. 'You can hardly call that a missing person, boy,' I told him, 'not *missing*, not with a note for the milkman an' all. That's a lady probably got fed up with the sight of you,' I said. Just joking, of course. I know Harry well. He's a worrier, Harry is.''

''Tell me what he worries about,'' Webber said.

NINE

Thelma Fronefield changed trains on the underground at Tottenham Court Road from the Northern to the Central Line and only finally relaxed when she was quite sure that she was travelling west to Notting Hill Gate and not east to the unknown wilderness of the outer suburbs. Her home in Edgware she didn't consider a suburb. Until this recent upheaval it had been the centre of her civilised world and she had fully intended spending the night there in the comfort of her own bed, and would have done if it hadn't been for the impossible behavior of her sister Rose. She would never have succumbed, but the lure of a pleasant evening of bridge had been too much. She might have known that such a thing would have been impossible. God knows where Rose found her ghastly friends, drinking Lionel's whisky out of her best crystal glasses and getting all the best hands. She had behaved beautifully, Thelma told herself. She might even have stayed and slept in her own bed if Rose hadn't broken a glass during the washing-up and then given her a lecture on Christian Science.

She caught the last tube train back to Kensington and the gallery.

At Bond Street, a lot of passengers left the carriage and a group of well-dressed black youths got in and sat opposite her, laughing and pushing each other. She saw the reflection of her smiling face in the window; smiling, not because she could hear a word of their conversation over the noise of the train, but smiling to show them she wasn't hostile, like a cat rolling over submissively on its back. She stopped smiling in case they should think it was an open invitation to rape. She was too old to be raped. No, she wasn't, the papers were full of it, old ladies of eighty, and none of them even wearing a full-length mink coat. She drew it closer round her. Three more stations and she would be safe. She considered getting out at the next one but a few more late passengers got in and she felt better. With the safety of more people around her she imagined herself alone again with the menace of the black youths threatening her with flick knives, like she had read about in the grim subway trains of New York. She pictured herself in the dock, in her dark grey with a touch of white somewhere. "My Lord, I never even heard the shots. . . . Yes, I must have taken the gun from my handbag, but if I am guilty then I am proud of it! As proud as a soldier fighting for the Queen of England."

With relief she brought her thoughts back to reality. The gun wasn't in her handbag, it was still in the drawer of the bedside table where she found it wrapped in a pair of Joseph's socks, long ago. He had hidden it there as a vain-glorious gesture against burglars. Both Joseph and Ruth had forgotten it, but Thelma was a compulsive tidier of drawers. It probably wasn't even loaded.

At Notting Hill Gate the black boys left the train without a backward glance at her, running and laughing along the platform and throwing away the wrappings of their chocolate bars. They raced up the moving escalator and out of her life, leaving her to let it carry her up more decorously into the safety of North Kensington. In a most satisfactory surge of pleasure, she felt she had routed them. In ten minutes she would be safe in the gallery.

* * *

In the basement room of the gallery, Benjamin and April Schittski had drawn the thick curtains across the grubby window that looked out onto the tiny area holding the dustbins and stacks of old crates and broken picture frames. A small flight of stones steps led up to the iron railings and the squeaky gate which opened on to the badly lighted pavement of Pig Lane. If it hadn't been for Thelma Fronefield's honesty they would already have left for Suffolk. Thelma had found the silk square with the pattern of horses and hounds and bridles which she had remembered as belonging to April. Not Hermes, but a good quality silk. She had telephoned the Norland. Yes, she had told Dr. Lamb, they could certainly pick it up or she would post it to them. If they wanted to collect it, then it would be best to do so tomorrow morning, say, ten-thirty. She should be back by then. She was, she explained, spending the night with her sister Rose in Edgware.

The basement lock was as easy for Benjamin to open as if he had his own key. Only the shriek of the rusty hinges, worse even than the gate, had given him a moment's discomfort. The trick was to open it quickly—a short shriek was always better than a prolonged, drawn-out howl.

A quick search of the gallery cupboards and the rooms upstairs satisfied him that they held no concealed masterpiece by Stanley Spencer. He was careful to use a torch and not to turn on any upstairs lights. In the musty basement he felt safer. The pictures were stacked six deep along the walls and piled in undisturbed mildew and dust on a table at the end of the room.

"My God, Ben, this place hasn't been touched for months. Only a fool would store anything decent down here."

"Unless that's what Ruth thought, too. She could have

slipped it in here carefully somewhere. A few days wouldn't hurt it."

Even as he said it he knew instinctively that he was wrong. But work was work and it took less time than he thought to finger through the stacks of canvases. Mostly rubbish, the accumulation of Joseph's scavanging, and things he must have bought in country sale-rooms in desperation, Benjamin thought. Knowing Joseph, some would eventually have been rescued, sent off to one of his restorers to be cleaned and tarted up for sale, probably at auction hoping to catch the gullible and unwary looking for bargains. The art world, on both sides of the Atlantic, was full of Josephs and their restorers. It genuinely saddened him.

The instant that he heard footsteps approaching the shop he switched off the light. It could have been any innocent passer-by but Benjamin was a professional and not given to taking risks. In the darkness of the basement, with his hand on April's arm, they both froze. The steps were a woman's and they stopped. A wild hope made him picture someone pausing to check the time or light a cigarette. The sound of a key in the lock of the door of the shop and the hope faded. The bloody woman had come back. A movement from April towards the basement door tightened his warning grip on her arm. The noise from the rusty hinges would scream through the building and she would certainly phone for the police. He didn't like the idea of being stopped by a cruising police car and questioned in the late night streets and she might easily catch a glimpse of them from the shop window. Benjamin had a great respect for the efficiency of cruising police cars.

"Wait till she goes upstairs," he breathed into April's ear. "If she comes down here hit her, but for Christ's sake try not to kill her."

He strained to hear every step and movement from upstairs, following the woman in his mind as clearly as if he were there beside her. He thanked God that he was a careful man and had left everything undisturbed.

Thelma locked and checked the safety chain of the shop door. She moved to the door of the basement stairs and stopped, with her hand turning on the handle. No, not tonight. She was tired after an evening with Rose and the trauma of the tube journey. The basement was always the same, smelly and safely locked with a Victorian key she could barely twist. She thought of making herself a hot drink in the kitchen and decided instead on the whisky she had so pointedly refused at the bridge table.

She paused at the foot of the steep stairs in the gallery. The paintings on the walls, she decided, looked, if anything, even more dull and drab in the faint light of the distant street lamp than they did in the day. No wonder no one had bought any of them, or for that matter had shown the slightest interest. Every day she had spoken to Ruth on the telephone and had to tell her the same depressing news. Ruth couldn't even make the calls herself. She had no telephone. What a terrible thing for a daughter to queue like a shop-girl at a phone-box and tell a mother to be patient. Interesting local contacts! What did she *mean*, interesting contacts? You could play with fire like that, chatting foolishly to spies from the Inland Revenue or Her Majesty's Customs and Excise. She washed her face and thought of the Queen smiling sweetly as she took Lionel's hand, a tiny woman with skin like a rose petal. The water gurgled away to the basement and in bed she drank the whisky, smoothed Nivea cream on her face and her elbows, and longed for Lionel.

In the basement, Benjamin heard the water and carefully eased back the curtains without a sound. In the top windows of a house on the opposite side of the street he watched the reflection of her bedroom light and saw it go out. It had been a long time since April had eaten dinner. He glared at her as she rustled the paper on a chocolate bar. Guiltily, she turned to throw the wrapping away and, catching a nail on a picture frame with her sleeve, she pulled a whole pile of pictures towards her. They fell to the floor in a cloud of dust and with the sound of a muffled explosion.

Thelma was not asleep, not really asleep. She shot out of her twilight doze and knew at once what had happened. The black gang had followed her home and waited until she had put her light out. What a stupid, conceited old woman she was to wear real mink on a tube train, the mink that Lionel had given her for their wedding anniversary. Emboldened by anger and the whisky, and with Joseph's gun in her hand, she flew down the stairs, an avenging fury in a baby-doll nightdress. They might have escaped her once and that was enough. Stupid, ignorant, giggling boys, she would put the fear of a vengeful God into them and teach them a lesson they would remember for the rest of their law-abiding lives. She saw herself herding them upstairs at gunpoint—how should they know it wasn't loaded?—saw them tearful and contrite while she telephoned for the police.

For once Benjamin's calm had deserted him and frozen him into appalled immobility. Thelma shot into the basement and fell headlong over the pile of canvases before she could reach for the light switch. For an instant, she saw a figure dimly against the glimmer from the window with an arm raised to strike or stab her. The full force of April's backhand was dissipated as Thelma lurched forward over the paintings but the blow blinded her with tears and frenzied anger. She pressed the trigger again and again. The gun exploded with an incredible noise in the small room. Now deaf as well as blind, she heard faintly the wild shriek of the rusty hinges and her last thought as she lost consciousness was a prayer of gratitude that she had at least taken one of them with her.

* * *

Webber and Mrs. Thomas sat on a wooden bench in the tree-lined courtyard of the hospital and waited for Ruth. She had been grateful for their offer to drive her up to London, but whether from shock or some private reason of her own had been silent for most of the journey. It said a lot for Lizzie, Webber thought, that Ruth Greenwood was prepared to accept him without question. Her private business was her own affair, he had told her, and she could certainly not be held accountable for her husband's unorthodox bookkeeping. He wasn't at all sure that this was true and was relieved to hear her say that she had told no one else except her mother. Her Aunt Rose had been encouraging on the telephone—her mother's injury wasn't serious and the hospital thought she would be well enough to go home in a day or two.

"Coincidence?" Mrs. Thomas said. "This gallery business, I mean."

"I forget the exact figure, but something like a break-in every twenty minutes. That's the metropolitan average, I believe," Webber said. "So I suppose, yes, you could call it a coincidence if you wanted to. What time did she say visiting-time finished?"

"She caught the last half hour. It looks as if it's up."

Ruth's figure walking towards them across the tarmac looked small and vulnerable.

"She's going to be all right. She was lucky; she got a punch on the neck, that's all. She thinks the gun scared them off."

"I didn't know about the gun," Webber said, opening the car door for her.

"Oh no, look, I can easily walk. It's not far. Well, thank you. I shall have to stay up for a while, of course. I'll phone Mr. Coley and explain I'll have to see her settled at Edgware. No, I didn't know about the gun either; apparently she found it in a drawer. I remember telling Joe to get rid of it ages ago. I thought he had. The police don't like it but they seem to have accepted her explanation that she didn't know it was loaded. This lift is really very kind of you."

"Was she able to give them any sort of description?" Webber asked, guiding the car out into the traffic.

"She says it was a gang of black men she saw on the tube. They want her to look at some photographs when she's better."

"You sound doubtful," Webber said.

"She's still very shocked and she's always—well, she's always had a very lively imagination. She thinks they followed her home from the tube. She seems more worried about Auntie Rose than anything."

"What's wrong with Rose?" Mrs. Thomas asked.

"She's a Christian Scientist and I don't think Mummy is in the mood for it at the moment. She says Rose has got an answer for everything."

"Lucky old Rose," Webber said.

TEN

He was pleased to see a car drawing away from a parking meter in Pig Lane and unchivalrously stole it from a more cautious driver who had positioned himself to back carefully into the precious space.

"Sorry! Police," Webber said as the man got out to argue.

He followed Webber's nod in the direction of a policeman who was looking down into the basement area of the gallery. The man glared with frustration and drove away. The constable was watching a workman removing the temporary boarding before fitting a new lock. Ruth identified herself and went into the front entrance with Mrs. Thomas while Webber stayed to chat with the policeman. He was fresh-faced and young and his uniform, Webber noted with satisfaction, was reassuringly new. That morning, Webber had taken the trouble to telephone his old friend and ex-colleague, Detective Superintendent Snow at Scotland Yard. He hadn't expected Snow, with his newly-exhalted rank, to know the details of such an unimportant case, but at least he had been able to get from him the names of the local officers in charge of the gallery incident. This lad was a bit of unexpected luck; it might save him time and trouble at the local nick. He was careful to establish his status as a family friend, but a family friend with a knowledge of police procedure. The constable hadn't learned much in his brief service but he recognised authority.

"Well, that's good news, anyway, sir. The old lady shouldn't have used the gun, of course. I should think she'll get a good talking to. We could easily have had a few dead bodies on our hands." He sounded wistful.

"She must be a rotten shot," Webber said. "Difficult not to clip at least one of them down there, by the look of it. Unless she was firing blanks, of course?"

The boy policeman met his enquiring eyes frankly and Webber was touched to see him blush. He searched for his pipe and concentrated on filling it, only looking up at him again when he had lit it successfully.

"Quite right," he said. "You don't know who I am, and so why should you discuss police matters with someone who might be a villain—or a governor, for all you know?"

The boy nodded solemnly, wondering how he was going to word his report. Perhaps there was a special squad with offices who monitored cases at random?

"Forget it, I'm not official. I was a D.I. for a long time. I'm retired but I work privately sometimes." He glanced at the shop where Ruth and Mrs. Thomas were opening windows to let in fresh air and then down at the workman gathering up his tools in the basement. "This lot might just tie up with some inquiries I've been making in the country."

"I expect you could talk to Sergeant Benson at the station, sir. I came round with him that night."

Webber nodded. "I could, if he's got time and patience. Gets a bit cross sometimes, does he? Well, so will you one day, I dare say."

The workman delivered the new keys and they went in to give them to Ruth. While the boy was collecting her signature and wondering if it was right to accept Mrs. Thomas's offer of tea, Webber wandered down to the basement. He stayed there for about ten minutes, which was all he needed. When he came up, Ruth was upstairs and Mrs. Thomas was drinking tea with the constable, who had taken his helmet off and looked about sixteen. In fact, he was in his early twenties. Not good-looking in the accepted sense, it was a pleasant face, which he had inherited from his mother, who liked to think of herself as "*jolie laide*." His father, with Yorkshire bluntness, had once described them both as ugly but honest. Judging by the look of awe and respect on his face, Webber guessed that Mrs. Thomas had given the boy a lightning sketch of his past career, together with a wildly exaggerated account of his more spectacular successes.

"This young man is Andy Baldwin," Mrs. Thomas said, passing round a packet of Thelma's chocolate biscuits. "He lives in a Section House and the canteen food isn't very good."

Webber looked at her gratefully. He had paid the constable the compliment of treating him as grown up. Mrs. Thomas had gone straight to his stomach and turned him into a schoolboy again. Conversation was easy. Webber told him about the days when there were no canteens in police Section Houses and about hungry burglars who would sometimes be unable to resist eating everything they could find and then fell asleep, with their loot neatly packed at their feet. Andy chatted happily in such congenial company and they moved smoothly from food to fingerprints and the apparently superhuman efficiency of the Criminal Records Office at Scotland Yard. There was little at the end of it that Webber didn't know about the state of play in the police investigations, up to the moment, at least. Andy looked shocked when he eventually thought of glancing at his wristwatch. He stood up guiltily and adjusted the unfamiliar helmet, reluctantly allowing Mrs. Thomas to wipe some chocolate from the corner of his mouth before letting him rejoin the police force.

"A dear little chap," she said, gazing after him. "Like a little toy. He's going to see his Mam on Sunday."

"That's nice."

"A useful chat?" she asked.

"Yes." Webber wondered if he had himself been quite so naïve at Andy's age and decided that he had, only more so, and not so nice and trusting. "For the next week or so that 'dear little chap' of yours is going to walk over his ground looking with deep suspicion into all the corners where two or three black boys are gathered together and he won't find a thing. His Governor won't discourage him because it will be good experience for him."

"They didn't do it?"

"I shouldn't think so. More like Ruth's mum letting her imagination out for an airing. You heard young Andy, there were glove marks all round the door and quite a few on the canvas frames. I can't see kids on tube trains carrying gloves, and only a real old pro would know about rusty Victorian locks like that. No wonder none of the marks they did find down there were in the C.R.O. files. They'll turn out to be all L.A.s. Real bullets, though. Whoever it was, was lucky."

"L.A.s?"

"Legitimate access. Ruth's prints or her husband's or her mother's, if she ever went down there. Are you sure you'll be all right?" he asked Ruth, who had come downstairs.

"Well, there doesn't seem to be anything missing," she said. "At least, I think she only had five fur coats at the last count. Yes, of course, I will—I'm very grateful to both of you."

"You said you wouldn't go and see Victoria Varley," Webber said. "You didn't phone her either?"

"I couldn't trust myself; that's why I was so glad to speak to Lizzie. The wretched woman is probably off on a spending spree somewhere—with Joe's money."

"And you think that young Fellows has no idea where she is?"

Ruth shook her head firmly. "No, he's not very bright—all body and not much brain. He seems genuinely worried about her, though, and I think he's frightened, too."

"I wonder why?" Webber said. "He says he wasn't with her the night your husband died. Do you think he's hiding something? About the money, I mean?"

Ruth sat at the desk and considered. So much had happened that it seemed difficult to get her thoughts in order or to absorb new ones. She smoothed the folded silk scarf that lay next to the old basement lock the workman had left. She thought of Harry Fellows being sent round by the vicar and telling her that she needn't worry about any parish duties, standing and talking to her in the pocket handkerchief of the cottage garden and offering to tidy it up for her. And of Joan

Coley waving good morning to them so vigorously that she had nearly fallen off her rattling old bicycle.

"No, I think he's just a silly country kid and a bit stage struck, only these days it's television, isn't it? He knows every word of that television advertisement she does for tinned beer or whatever it is."

The world, Webber thought, seemed to be full of naïve young men.

"If he knew anything about Joe's money, he'd be more likely helping her to spend it somewhere. I think she must be a really horrible woman. You mustn't forget your scarf; it's pretty."

"It's not mine," Mrs. Thomas said. "It must belong to your mother."

Ruth held it up so that the folds fell open. "No, it's not Mummy's, she hates horses. She'd never wear this."

As they left, Webber said, "I don't want to worry your mother, not when she's unwell. Perhaps I might see her later when you've got her settled. Does she like chocolate?"

"I shouldn't bother, it's bad for her figure. Besides, she might think you're a potential suitor; she's at an awkward age."

It was Mrs. Thomas's private opinion that Webber was, too, but she kept the thought to herself.

"I suppose a lot of people you get in the gallery are American?" he said.

"Yes, some. Not all that many. Our stuff doesn't appeal to them very much, I'm afraid."

"I'll keep in touch," Mrs. Thomas said. "That young policeman said he'd look in on you, too."

"He's very active." Webber smiled. "It's probably his first job."

"Last week," Mrs. Thomas said, with unexpected vehemence, "he found a pedigree dog—*and* got a reward."

* * *

At the Glockemara, where they had so often stayed, she was down to breakfast before Webber next morning.

"Just boiled eggs?" the waiter said. "As usual, and, yes, I'll see they're not too hard. Shall I order for Mr. Webber?"

"He'll have his usual too, everything except potatoes and you know he doesn't like—"

"Doesn't like his bacon underdone, I remember. I *thought* he'd lost a little weight. Shall I put a few potatoes on for luck?"

"Don't you dare, young James," Webber said, sitting heavily and glowing from his shave. "I must have something to salve my conscience."

Young James was white-haired and probably well over eighty. The hotel kept him on out of kindness and because a surprising number of the old customers asked about him and expected him to be there. He liked Mrs. Thomas and Mr. Webber. In the past he had often wondered about them and their relationship, and it had defeated him. They didn't fit neatly into any of his standard pigeon-holes and he liked that because there were very few mysteries left in his life. It must be the sunset of an old affair, he thought, Mr. Webber respectably married and only able to meet her here when times were right. Most passion long-since spent, but a true and deep affection. It was touching, he thought, to see her buttering his toast for him.

In fact, she was scraping some of it off—bacon and eggs and sausages and fried bread and God knows what else was quite enough of a treat for one morning. Butter was tempting the devil.

"And you think you'll find her there?" she asked.

"Yes, either there at the flat in Oakley Street or perhaps her agent has got her a job of some sort. Betsey says she still gets the odd bits in films. She could be anywhere. At least I might be able to contact her. Are you sure you don't want to come?''

''No, you're best on your own.''

''What'll you do?''

''I can go to the travel agency and get a refund on your holiday, for one thing.''

''So soon? I might come back with twenty thousand pounds in notes and her apology for being so daft.''

''But you don't think so.''

''No, she's only got to sit tight and deny that she ever saw it.''

''And Ruth can come back to those awful pictures and whistle for it.''

''Not very exciting, are they? I'd rather have the one that Betsey bought from Victoria Varley. I like a bit of life and colour. I wonder what the old man copied it from? Betsey says a magazine or a postcard. Certainly it wasn't in Spencer's catalogue, and why should the old man have copied an unrecorded painting of Stanley Spencer's in Wangford, of all places? The man practically never left his own village.''

''I wasn't going to mention it until later,'' Mrs. Thomas said, folding her napkin carefully, ''but he did. Stanley Spencer married his first wife at Wangford and spent his honeymoon there. I think James is waiting to clear the table.''

ELEVEN

In the hall, while James shuffled off to fetch his raincoat from the cloakroom, Webber said, "I thought I'd been through that catalogue carefully." He made a rueful mouth at his carelessness.

"I missed it too—at first. There's a lot to look at. I went through it again last night. There's a long introduction as well as all the reproductions of his paintings. He liked Wangford; it had happy memories for him. He did some painting there, too."

He shrugged himself into the raincoat and grinned. "So there could be a genuine Spencer floating round the village somewhere for the old man to copy. No wonder Betsey seemed a bit reluctant to lend you the catalogue. Once a dealer! Not that you can blame him, I suppose. I'll bet he hoped we might miss the Wangford connection."

"Which you did."

"Which I did. I'm getting old."

James made sympathetic clucking noises as he brushed Webber's coat with a tremulous hand.

"I've no idea how long I shall be. We can always phone in and leave messages here as usual. Will that be all right with you, James?"

"Certainly, sir, madam, I'm always here."

"Good. Well, then, I expect you'll do some shopping," Webber said. "Don't spend all your money."

"You've got the address?"

"Yes, the flat and the theatre agent. Take care, love." He pecked her lightly on the cheek and was gone.

"The rain looks as if it's settling in again, I'm afraid, madam. I'm glad he ate all his potatoes," James said.

Oakley Street runs in a gentle curve from the King's Road in Chelsea down to the Thames and the splendour of the Albert Bridge. The houses, once the homes of respectable Victorian families, have long since become a warren of flats and bed-sitting rooms.

"Oh, do come into the office. You can leave your coat in the hall and it can drip away quite happily. It will be quite safe there. Isn't this weather beastly? We always seem to get the worst of it in Oakley Street." The woman spoke as if, only a few yards away, the sun was always shining on the King's Road and down on the river.

The bell marked "Varley" had remained unanswered and he had tried the one marked "Enquiries."

"Do sit down. I call it the office but it's really our sitting-room, as you can see."

A tired-looking man, presumably her husband, was writing a letter at a desk. He glanced up at Webber, nodded, and went on writing. Webber handed the woman his card.

"Dear me—a Detective Inspector!"

"I was. I'm retired," Webber assured her quickly, and took advantage of the moment to explain why he had rung the bell marked "Enquiries." " . . . so, it seemed sensible to see if she had simply decided to come up to her flat here in London, or, if not, to see if anyone here—yourselves, for instance—might know where she is? Has she been with you long, here in this house?"

In the silence which followed her husband folded his unfinished letter and took time with the cap of his fountain pen.

"No and yes," he said.

He sounded like a schoolmaster, Webber thought, a schoolmaster long since retired and starved of intelligent questions.

"The answers, Inspector, are: no, we don't know where Miss Varley is at the moment, but that is certainly not unusual—ladies in the theatrical profession are, as I'm sure you know, of a peripatetic nature. Her flat here is now, I understand, more of a *pied-à-terre* than her permanent home. And: yes, she has been with us for many years—at a peppercorn rent, I may say." He smiled sadly at his wife over his half-moon glasses—a smile reserved for a favourite pupil.

"Do you have a key to Miss Varley's flat?" Webber asked him.

"We have keys to all our flats; it's a question of fire regulations."

"That's what I thought. I told you that I am no longer a serving policeman. I have no authority at all, but I think you ought to consider just looking to make sure that everything is as it should be with her. I don't want to upset your wife but people do get taken ill. There are such things as heart attacks."

The flat was at the top of the house. A sitting-room, a bedroom with a tiny bathroom, and kitchen, all leading off the top landing. They had once been servants' bedrooms.

"Perhaps, my dear, you'd better stay outside while Mr. Webber and I see that everything is in order. I'm sure it will be."

The sitting-room was shabby but tidy. It smelled of carpet and the dust which lay undisturbed on the furniture. The bedroom was tidy, too. Only the dust smelled of stale scent, the same scent which in the bathroom was mixed with toothpaste and soap. The kitchen had no sign of anything sinister, either, except, Webber noted with interest, that a bowl of fruit on the sink had gone bad, the oranges and a lemon were covered with a thick white mould and some bananas were black and weeping a heady syrup. There wasn't much in the little refrigerator—half a small, cooked chicken still in its supermarket wrapping and a small dish of mixed, cooked vegetables. They all smelled sour and inedible. As he closed the fridge, the woman walked past them to the only door they hadn't opened. It was next to the bathroom and Webber knew it had to be the lavatory. She hesitated for a moment before pulling it roughly open and then turning to them with a face drained of colour.

"Goodness, what a relief! How silly of me. It was something you said, Mr. Webber, although, of course, it really would have been the most bizarre coincidence, not that coincidences don't happen I mean, but—"

"My dear, you mustn't distress yourself; it was all such a long time ago," the schoolmaster said.

Webber's face held only a polite professional enquiry.

"Miss Varley was married when she first came to us. Her husband had a heart attack. She discovered him there, on the lavatory—after some long time, I believe. Most distressing for her but the doctor and the inquest confirmed that it could have made no difference, he died almost within seconds, they said."

Webber nodded. "It does happen."

The Satyricon Travel Agency in Victoria had paint flaking on the outside of the shop and a young man with skin flaking on his nose inside. Neither prospect filled Mrs. Thomas with confidence. The place was far less imposing than its glossy brochure had suggested.

"I shall have to check with head office, I'm afraid," the

young man said at last, when confronted with the sad necessity of actually returning Webber's deposit.

He shot a miserable look into the back of the shop, where a bored-looking woman was typing viciously. "Five pounds cancellation fee," she said, and went back to her typing.

It was cheap at the price. Webber, she considered, had had a lucky escape. And now there was work for him. Better than any holiday.

Freed from responsibility, the youth made out her refund cheerfully enough.

"It's a shame he couldn't make it. I was in Tuscany myself last week and the sun was really hot."

"I can see. Well, let's hope the weather here will pick up."

"Perhaps, later on, Mr. Webber might like one of our fine-art holidays? We do a special guided tour of Florence—all the galleries and museums. A friend of mine went last year and—"

"Shut up, Gerald, for Christ's sake, and just give her the cheque," the bored woman said to her typewriter.

"Thank you." Mrs. Thomas smiled at him graciously and put the cheque carefully into her handbag. "And tell your head office not to swear, it lowers the tone. I wonder if you could direct me to the Tate Gallery?"

Webber had a jolly reception at Victoria Varley's agent's office. In fact, Mr. Murreyfield seemed genuinely pleased to see him. He seemed pleased with life in general.

"Let's try The Bell. If we get in early we can get a quiet seat in the corner and the bar food's not too bad."

He was overweight and overjovial. Webber had known many like him and they had nearly all been con men. Murreyfield made no attempt to pay for the shepherd's pie or the beer.

"Oh yes, for many years now. Not only a client, dear boy, but a personal friend, too, yes, indeed. Victoria and I are very close. A wonderful actress. That's just the thing dear boy: quality. There's nothing like quality—star quality."

"But not for some time, I think?"

"My dear man, you can hardly expect me to agree with that. Ungallant, Mr. Webber, ungallant! And, I assure you, not true."

He attacked the shepherd's pie eagerly, his lips wet with indignation and gravy. It gave Webber a chance to tell him that Victoria had disappeared from her home in Flaxfield and that she had not been seen in the Oakley Street flat for some time, either.

"There is no suggestion of anything wrong in Flaxfield or up here, it's just that she never told anyone she was going away. It seemed to me that if anyone might know where she is, then you would be the most likely."

"Well, I don't." Victoria's agent wiped his plate clean with the last piece of his bread. "I bloody well don't." He didn't say it aggressively but quietly as someone who hears bad news. His jovial manner had quite gone.

"Pity," Webber said. "That would have been a nice, tidy explanation. I rather hoped you had fixed her up with a job of some sort, a few days' filming, perhaps. I can't face another pint at lunch time. Will you join me in a whisky?"

They drank it in silence and Webber waited for the large measure to help the beer loosen the man up. His own glass held only ginger ale.

"Your card said 'Inspector,' " Murreyfield said accusingly. "I didn't know you were retired."

"I know. A bit of a cheat. I realised that you were a busy man. The card's useful sometimes. No, I'm just a neighbour, nothing official."

"Nothing to worry about, dear boy." Murreyfield seemed

to be convincing himself as much as Webber. "I saw her—when? Oh, I don't know. I can look in my diary. I've been very busy lately, not long ago, anyway. Look, this is all rather confidential, dear boy. I don't discuss clients' private affairs but I can see you're worried. You see, in a way, you were right—Victoria is not the easiest client I've got on my books. Parts for women of her age don't grow on trees, you know. But I promise you she's all right. Yes, yes, that's just the thing—she'll have skipped off for a bit of a break somewhere. The excitement, I expect."

"The excitement?"

"Keep it to yourself, of course, but the fact is that she's come into a little money. I didn't ask questions, you know, not my business. That's just the thing, not my business. She'll be back, I'm quite sure of it. I know Victoria."

Webber had shaken hands with many people through the years. It never bothered him, it was part of the job. He found it useful. You shook hands and they relaxed.

"You've been very helpful, Mr. Murreyfield. Her friends will be very relieved. When she gets in touch I'd be most grateful if you could find time to ring me? Going to invest it for her, were you?"

TWELVE

"And was he?" Mrs. Thomas asked, settling herself comfortably and looking around the restaurant with interest.

"Was he what?" A new restaurant was always an adventure and Webber studied the menu with care.

"Going to invest it for her?"

"I thought you meant was he a con man. Shall we be devils and try the steak? It should be tender at that price."

It was only the idea of a new restaurant that attracted him, she thought, not the food, since he inevitably chose steak. She comforted herself with the knowledge that her cooking had spoiled him. They both chose steak, and she waited patiently for him to tell her his day.

"Our friend Mr. Murreyfield was angling for some of her money to invest in a new play," he said.

"Can agents do that?"

"He runs a company that does."

"She doesn't sound the flighty type, not someone you could persuade to part with money easily."

"He was angling, I said. The bait was a good part in the play for her. The price was fifteen thousand pounds."

"Fifteen thousand pounds?"

"That's what he said."

"And she said she'd come into a bit of money?"

"Yes."

"But she didn't say how?"

"No."

"Greenwood's money or most of it. It must be."

"Yes, I should think so. Murreyfield hasn't seen any of it yet, so he couldn't say whether it was to be cash or not."

"Was the play any good, I wonder?"

"I wouldn't even know if I read it. My guess is that Murreyfield would have used just enough of the money to get her the part and pocketed the rest. It is just a guess but I'm better at villains than plays."

"You don't think that she's parted with it already?"

"And boyo pushed her in the river one night? No, he was

too upset that she might have had second thoughts. With a few drinks inside him he said that it was all fixed up. He had dinner with the people doing the play. Victoria was supposed to phone him that night at ten o'clock to hear whether they wanted her or not. She never phoned. That was the night Coley had his dinner party. No, he's worried alright. He's not that good an actor, although he told me that's how he started."

"And finished up as a con man."

"Well, as a theatrical agent. I expect there are some good agents but I don't think he's one of them. They're taking their time with the food, aren't they?"

"You seem to have had quite a long chat with him."

"I mentioned friends in high places," Webber said. "As it happened, I'd arranged to see Ted Snow at the Yard this afternoon, anyway. That seemed to concentrate Mr. Murreyfield's mind wonderfully. Ah, here we are. Shall we have some wine?"

She looked at her plate dubiously. "Let's try it first. The last time you asked Ted for help you both got into trouble."

"He's very grand now, got his own office. Superintendents get a carpet and an armchair. He owes me a few favours remember; it wasn't a problem. How is your steak?"

"The same as yours, by the look of it. Waiter!"

"I hope you're not going to make a fuss." For a brave man Webber could be a terrible coward.

"No, not a fuss, but I want to hear about Ted and I want to enjoy it. I don't like con tricks any more than you do.

"I thought I'd just explain why we're leaving"—she smiled kindly at the young waiter—"because I haven't got time to explain it to the chef. Detective Inspector Webber has had a very tiring day—so have I—and I'm sure you'll understand why we don't feel like eating burnt, tough steak and limp, soggy chips swimming in lukewarm grease. Not your fault, my love, just tell the chef. I wish I had the time to tell him myself.''

Webber was already waiting for her at the door. ''We could have ordered something else,'' he said resignedly.

''Fish and chips just round the corner. We should have gone there in the first place.''

She was right, as always, he thought. About food, anyway.

They were welcomed as old friends, and spoiled with the best restaurant meal in the world, ten seconds from the fryer in the kitchen to the plates in front of them.

''And we'll have a bottle of the Sancerre, please,'' Webber ordered, without consulting her.

''Better?'' she asked, smiling round the familiar room.

''Certainly, you horrible, embarrassing woman.''

''So, did your Mr. Murreyfield rate a mention in the records at the Yard?''

''I didn't go to see Ted about him, although, as a matter of fact, we did do a check on him while I was there. No, nothing. He's just a little crook with no billing. No, I'd sent Ted a chocolate wrapper I found behind some canvases in the gallery basement. You didn't really think I had planned to seduce Ruth's mother with chocolate, did you?''

''Go on, and don't use so much salt.''

''It was just a chance; there might have been some prints on it and they might have been on file. Criminal Records in thc Yard's new building is really very impressive, Lizzie. It's all on one complete floor now and they've had to strengthen it to bear the weight, there's a special document-conveyor system with—''

''What made you think you'd find any prints? You said you thought whoever it was wore gloves.''

''They wrap things like chocolate bars very well these days; even without gloves it's difficult to get at them. I thought it was a chance.''

"And was it?"

"Yes, there were prints on it. Lizzie, this is so *good*. Thank God we decided to leave that other ghastly place."

"Were they on file at the Yard?"

He sighed. "No, no luck. Isn't that sad? Oh well. Nice clear prints, too."

"Anybody could have dropped it."

"Sure. Silly not to check though. I asked Ruth if they had many American customers, remember? Well, this wrapper was American, something called a Hershey Bar. They're not sold over here, I believe."

"American troops? They have their own shops. What do they call them?"

"PX, I think. Something like that. Sure, well, that narrows it down a bit—an American serviceman with no criminal record."

When he grinned, she thought he looked very boyish and quite lovely. He poured the wine into their glasses, squinting at them carefully to make sure neither had more than its share, something they always did with good wine.

"Sometimes I think that even if I'd stayed on in the force I'd never have rated an armchair and a carpet."

"If you're fishing for compliments, forget it. Or ask Ted; he'd tell you. How is he?"

"He's fine. And Betty and the kids. Alan's at Cambridge—he got his scholarship. No, Ted's all right. I was lucky to catch him. He's away a lot. Superintendents get all the nice murder jobs. He nips off all over the place, whenever anyone calls in the Yard."

"Envious?"

"No, not really. He doesn't see much of Betty and the kids and he says he misses the garden. He's a rotten gardener. I didn't tell him that though. Not much of a home life for him."

She felt ridiculously pleased, taking it as his way of comparing Ted's lot unfavourably with his own. That was what he had meant her to think. She knew better than to pursue it.

"Do you think Victoria is dead?"

He was less scrupulous in taking advantage. "What about a few more chips? We could share a portion? Half each?"

"Half each."

"Thank you." He sipped his wine, tasting and enjoying it. "I didn't think Greenwood's death was as odd as you did, and quite honestly it wasn't, either," he said defensively. "I reckon that I was quite right not to get a sniff of something fishy about it. People die decently of heart attacks all the time. Sarah Collins has laid out at least two of them in the village since then and they didn't get your hackles up, not even a whisker. Why? No, don't answer that. You know, Lizzie, you're just like one of those dogs you see on television, the ones they train to sniff out drugs and bombs, bounding all over the suitcases at airports and grinning all over their faces."

"I shall take that as a compliment. Go on."

"You were meant to. Then you butter up silly old Gough and find out—"

"He's not all that silly."

"And find out what Greenwood was doing in Wangford—how could you try and deport me to a land where they can't cook fish and chips?—then you zoom in on a bereaved old woman, uninvited."

"Teasdale is younger than I am. She only looks older. And I was invited in nice and tidy."

"You take crafty old Betsey with you, not only because he gives you a lift but because he might get some idea of what Greenwood was after."

She was genuinely shocked. ''Oh, come on! Crafty? You love him, you said so.''

''Yes, I do. A nice, gentle old pussy-cat, my friend, your son-in-law, and an antique dealer. I'm not disparaging him, he was only doing his job; if you think you might be on to something you don't tell everyone about it.''

''Like policemen?''

''Well, perhaps crafty wasn't quite the right word. Let's say astute. Anyway, clever enough to keep quiet about Stanley Spencer until he could see it was a copy. You guessed he was on to something, though, didn't you, right from the beginning?''

''I knew he'd tell me in his own good time and anyway the important thing was the link with Victoria Varley.''

Webber looked regretfully at his empty plate and poured the last of the wine meticulously. ''Yes, that was interesting. Even more interesting though was what she did next. Betsey tells her that the Toby Jug was quite valuable so she gives it back to Mrs. Teasdale but she sells the painting to Betsey. Now, why should she do that? Shall we try the apple crumble?''

''Yes, all right, without cream, and you tell me why.''

''Let's guess. She didn't want old mother Teasdale kicking up a fuss and opening up the Greenwood visit again.''

''Then why sell the painting?''

It was a civilised restaurant and the anti-smoking fanatics had long ago abandoned it as beyond redemption. Webber filled his pipe and lit it luxuriously. ''Well, we might as well go on guessing. Greenwood was a picture man, right? So it's fair to assume that it was the painting he was interested in, not the Toby Jug. Like Betsey, he saw the Polaroid snapshot. He couldn't judge it properly by that any more than Betsey could, but it was enough to send him off to Victoria Varley's place.''

"Where he asks to use the lavatory and dies on it."

"Hang on, you were the one who didn't like that set-up, so let's forget the lavatory. Let's say he introduces himself quite openly as a respectable dealer, that he's seen a photograph of a painting he might be interested in and offers to buy it. We don't have to guess what he offered for it."

"A copy like that wouldn't fool a London dealer."

"Do you remember what Betsey said? 'In a poor light you could be looking at a fortune.' Oh good! Apple crumble."

"Start eating it from the outside or you'll burn yourself. Go on."

"It's a theory, but it fits. The medical evidence was clear enough—sudden shock and he could have gone any time. Even if he believed he was looking at a real Spencer for only a few seconds, that would have been enough."

They ate the steaming-hot food carefully and in silence until he used his napkin gratefully and waited for her to finish, too.

"And?" she said.

"She tries to revive him—let's allow her that anyway—but he's gone. She'd have to try and find out where he lived, or his phone number. You can't leave a total stranger lying around dead so she goes through his pockets. Reasonable?"

"Yes, reasonable. She finds that they're stuffed with twenty thousand pounds in cash and the temptation is too much for her."

"Something like that."

"It still doesn't explain why she returned the Toby Jug but sold Betsey the picture."

"The jug really was worth something. Victoria wanted no fuss and no awkward questions. She wanted to establish herself as an honest woman. After all, she had just stolen twenty thousand pounds. She could afford to forget a Toby Jug."

"And the picture?"

"I very much doubt that Greenwood would have told her what he thought about it, good or bad. She thought it was just a poor daub painted by a doddering old man and she was right, it is. Mrs. Teasdale knew that, too. She wasn't likely to get upset if Victoria sold that. The Toby was different."

"You've left him dead on the floor. How does he get on the lavatory?"

"I think she put him there. She wanted his visit to have nothing to do with antiques; that could open up the scene and expose her to a whole lot of questions. His visit was to be purely for personal reasons."

"You make her sound very bright, a quick thinker."

"She didn't have to think much."

Webber told her about his visit to Victoria's flat in Oakley Street.

"She remembered how her own husband had died in the lavatory and it gave her the idea. Which makes it all rather different, doesn't it?" he said.

"These people—in Oakley Street—what did you think of them?"

"As honest as most people, a bit more than most, perhaps. But then I thought that about Victoria."

"She must have been quite strong to drag a corpse to the lavatory all by herself."

"Unless Harry Fellows helped her," Webber said.

THIRTEEN

In the car, on the way home to Suffolk, they didn't talk much. It was one of the things he liked about her—she knew when he wanted to be quiet and think. Not until they had left London far behind them did he begin to relax, knowing that once they had pushed their way through the slow traffic of Essex they would be back in the county of his youth, the place where he could breathe easily and where he had been born. Sometimes he marvelled that she had adapted so well to a part of the country so different from the soft, rolling hills of Wales. It had never been a problem for her, but she had no intention of embarrassing him. Wherever Webber was, she felt at home.

At Marlesford he turned north off the main road into a maze of side roads and country lanes which would lead them to Flaxfield. Beyond Great Glenham, they stopped on a rise of the road—which was known proudly as a hill by the local people—and looked out over the fields and farms under the huge dome of the East Anglian sky.

"Will you miss your holiday in Italy?"

"Don't be daft. Shall we stretch our legs?"

It was, he thought, as good a non-committal reply as any. The truth was that as far as his personal life was concerned he was never quite sure whether his decisions were his own or whether in some subtle way she had influenced, or even manipulated him. He had spent a large part of his career talking to people and trying to guess the thoughts and motives behind their words. He was very grateful that Lizzie had never taken to crime.

They found a broken piece of ancient farm machinery and sat on the warm grass to lean against it.

"You didn't fancy going out to Edgware to see Ruth's mother, then?"

"Not much," he said. "I don't think she knows any more than we do already. It's not worth stopping anywhere for food now, is it?"

"I'll make an omelette or something at home."

"That's what I thought. Ruth says she's coming to Flaxfield again when she's got her mother settled. That doesn't look as though she's got a guilty conscience."

"I can't see Ruth doing anything stupid," Mrs. Thomas said thoughtfully. "She's not the type. But then, you say there is no such thing as a type."

"Twenty thousand pounds in notes is a lot of money; quite nice people have killed for much less than that."

"We'd never have known about the money if Ruth hadn't told me. She wanted to talk. She told me when we stopped for tea one day when I was helping her clean the cottage. You do think Victoria is dead, then?"

"Either dead or sunning herself in Spain or somewhere."

"But you don't think so."

"No, no, I don't. Betsey says she's infatuated with young Fellows. People don't go off on their own when they're in love, or even if they think they are, and I'm damn sure she wouldn't miss the chance of making a come-back in the theatre, even if it was only a small part."

"London's a big city," she said. "She wouldn't be the first one to disappear in that place. Suppose the people in

Chelsea found out about the money. You said they had a key to her flat."

"Somehow I can't see them leaving fruit to rot and food in the fridge." He sighed and shifted his weight against the uncomfortable ironwork. "Unless, of course, they're much cleverer than they seemed to be. I did wonder, I must admit. In fact just for a laugh I checked them out with C.R.O.s, too."

"You kept Ted busy."

"He's my lovely man, always was. I checked Harry Fellows out as well. Nothing. Nothing on anybody," he said sadly.

"Did you tell Ted about the money?"

"I told him enough to let him see I was serious. Don't worry, I wouldn't embarrass you over something Ruth told you in confidence. Anyway, it's not an official enquiry. There's a lot to be said for being retired. Victoria Varley is missing, that's all. Actresses move around. She's done it before. Women go missing all over England. The police do something—what they can, anyway—if they have something really solid to go on. Like a dead body, for instance, and God knows they get enough of those to keep them busy."

"Has anybody had a look inside her house?"

"Sergeant Burnstead did; Harry Fellows asked him to. Burnstead says he's a worrier. He doesn't believe she'd just have gone off without saying anything to him. The place was just as it should be, everything turned off at the mains. Harry has a key she let him use. There was a note for the milk man in her handwriting: 'No milk until further notice.' Let's go home; I'm hungry." He helped her up.

"I've been thinking," she said. "An American might not get a mention in Scotland Yard's C.R.O.s, but he could have a record in America, couldn't he?"

Webber glanced at her appreciatively. It was something he

had already thought of himself. "I mentioned it to Ted. He's going to check the prints on the chocolate wrapper with the FBI. The Yanks are very fussy about the people they accept in their forces, but it's worth a try."

They stood looking for a moment out over the fields, neatly tidied by hedgerows and the patches of trees where the land was too poor for the plough.

"You're right, Lizzie," he said. "London *is* a big place—but not as big as Suffolk."

FOURTEEN

"And this is the kitchen," Mr. Gough said, opening the door with a flourish.

April Schittski looked at it with disbelief bordering on horror. When Ben had suggested renting a house rather than staying at the local pub—which had the nerve to call itself an hotel—she had pictured gracious living in the kind of old-world English charm she had seen so often on television.

Benjamin Lamb followed them and seemed less appalled than she did. Gough mistook the silence for approval.

"This is one of our better properties," he said proudly.

April turned on the tap over the stone sink. A stream of brown water did nothing to raise her spirits.

"Leave it on; it soon runs clear," Gough said cheerfully. "You'll find everything works perfectly and, as you've seen, the rooms are fully and—if I may say so—quite pleasantly furnished." He decided not to mention the outside lavatory at the bottom of the garden. Main sewers had not reached every part of Flaxfield yet.

April wandered out of the kitchen in disgust and left them discussing the rent and signing the inventory. She could see that Ben had decided to take it and she knew better than to object. She could easily have cried, but released her frustration and anger by carrying the suitcases upstairs and starting to unpack in a bedroom smelling of damp and the remains of last winter's apples, which she found stored in the wardrobe. The voices of the men drifted up from below, drowned by the rumbling of the water tank in the attic above her head, industriously cleaning itself of rust.

"From Dallas!" Gough was saying. "How interesting." He wondered if there were any extras he could plausibly add to the rent they had already agreed and decided regretfully that there were limits even for Americans.

Benjamin had chosen Dallas deliberately—it was no good fishing without decent bait. It was the reason he had not protested at the outrageous money the oily old sod was asking for the house. He had lived long enough in America to be able to assume a quite passable accent when he wanted to and April could speak for herself, but not too much, he hoped.

"I can give you a cheque on an English bank," he said. "I have a London account. Mrs. Lamb and I often come over. We are both very fond of English antiques and I guess we know enough to save money buying them over here and not in the States. Suffolk is a part of your country I confess we haven't had the pleasure of visiting before. We are looking forward to it."

Gough beamed at him fondly. "An English bank. Yes, certainly, no trouble at all. Trust, my dear doctor, goodwill and trust. It is what I have always believed in. Yes, just here on the bottom, if you would be so kind and I will witness it for you. Antiques, yes, indeed. And you are quite right—Suffolk, I have always said, has been largely neglected. We do get tourists of course, but they mostly come in coach parties to look at the churches." He folded the lease carefully and slid it into the warm welcome of his inside jacket pocket like a trout swallowing a fat fly. "As one of the oldest established firms in East Anglia," he began with quiet sincerity, "we don't only deal in real estate, we have many contacts in the world of fine art. Our auction rooms, although I say it myself, are—"

"Would somebody," April said icily, in the doorway, "kindly tell me where I can find the john?"

"Come through to the garden, Mr. Webber, if you've got a moment. I've found something got me real worried."

Webber dutifully followed Sergeant Burnstead from the front office—which was the nerve centre of law and order in Flaxfield—through his kitchen, where the children stopped screaming and Burnstead's wife smiled to him through a thicket of uncombed hair while she ladled baked beans over great doorsteps of toast. Webber had been passing the police station on his way to the common for his early morning walk. Burnstead's broad back without his tunic showed his braces in an unexpected display of bright red. Webber guessed them to be a Christmas present, from the children perhaps. He found it difficult to associate Mrs. Burnstead with an avant garde taste in braces.

The tidy rows of early vegetables and salads ended with a neat line of beansticks and beyond that the flowers that Burnstead liked to cut for the counter in his office. They stood looking at the horror in silence.

"It must have happened very quickly," Burnstead said. "I was busy all day yesterday, so I never got down here."

"Some time in the last twenty-four hours then?"

Burnstead nodded sadly. "That turned my stomach right over, Mr. Webber. Greenfly, yes, but not blackfly. I've never had blackfly on the roses before."

Even though there was no strength in the sun and there was a fresh breeze from the common, Webber was surprised to find himself sweating. He dismissed his morbid thoughts and concentrated on the problem of the sergeant's plague. "You didn't have your runner beans down here last year, did you?"

"Up near the kitchen, but the missus said that took the light away and blocked her view."

"That's your trouble, then; beans and roses together always bring blackfly."

"You reckon?"

"They do in my garden, anyway. I've never seen it in any of the books, but they do. You can't do much about it this year except spray and pray."

Two of the older children had come out of the kitchen and were fighting fiercely and silently among the lettuces. Webber followed Burnstead up the path and watched him administer summary and unemotional justice.

"And it won't be just a tap next time?" he shouted after them as they fled laughing across the corner of the common towards the churchyard. "And don't you go pestering Mr. Fellows. He don't want kids round him all morning. You mind what I say, now!" The boy and girl stopped reluctantly, recognising a tone in their father's voice it would be unwise to disobey.

"Harry not like kids?"

"Oh, Harry's all right. He'd time-waste all day if he could. He makes kites for the kids. He's clever with his hands, is Harry. So 'tisn't only the children to blame, only that upsets the vicar—Harry not doing his work properly—so I've had him complaining. 'It's all very well, Vicar,' I told him, 'but I can't watch the little devils all day. You don't know what kids are like,' I said, 'you and Mrs. Coley not being blessed with any of your own.' I could have mentioned Mrs. Coley herself, if it comes to time-wasting with Harry, what with cups of tea and coffee all day and keeping him talking when he should be working, but, of course, I didn't. That wouldn't have sounded very nice and I wouldn't have meant it like that. There's no harm in it I'm sure. She's a nice woman and kind enough but just between you and me, Mr. Webber, I rèckon she's a silly old fool and so is the vicar, too, to my thinking. 'You're quite wrong about the children, Sergeant,' he told me. 'A priest has to think of everyone as his children.' I find it very difficult to argue with a man like that."

"He takes his job very seriously," Webber said mildly. "Harry hasn't heard from his friend Miss Varley, by any chance?"

"He's been watching too much old rubbish on the telly," Burnstead sighed. " 'Don't you think I'm busy enough, boy,' I said, 'without chasing after your lady friends for you?' She went off for six weeks last year doing some commercial or other in the Orkneys—fish fingers or someting—and forgot to cancel her milk, which at least she remembered to do this time."

"Was Harry here last year when she went off to the Orkneys?"

Burnstead furrowed his brow and concentrated. "No," he said at last. "No, that was spring and he didn't start working here until last summer. He joined the darts team when we were playing The Swan and that was late summer for certain. I don't know where he was before that."

"He's not local," Webber said. It was a statement, not a question. Both he and Burnstead had been born in Flaxfield. "Local," to them, had a very definite circumscription. On the few occasions when Webber had spoken to Harry Fellows, he had found it difficult to place his accent. Uneducated, certainly, and pleasant enough, with a countryman's soft burr, but not local.

"Truth is," said Burnstead, "I don't rightly know much about Harry. He's a great talker but he don't say much. He did say once that he was brought up in an orphanage. One of Mr. Coley's lame ducks, I reckon. He throws a clever dart, that I do know, though he don't seem so keen now as he used to be. That Miss Varley has wholly got under his skin."

"You think it was really serious, then?"

"On Harry's side, yes, it was. I can't speak for her, I never had any contact with her."

"How did he come to know her?"

"He's got one of the church cottages, over to Wangford way, that was near her and she got him on to doing a bit of gardening for her. He's a good worker, I'll say that. I'd offer you coffee, Mr. Webber, but time's getting on."

"My fault, sorry, I must get on, too. Keeping busy?"

"The usual—motor accidents, a punch-up in The King's Head last night, and larceny from a washing line."

They nodded aimiably as they parted. Burnstead watched Webber thoughtfully as he skirted the edge of the common and made his way towards the church. He wished that Webber wouldn't make him feel uneasy about his friendship with Harry. It wasn't even a real friendship; darts and beer, that's all. Useful to have an excuse to get away from the wife and the kids now and then.

Silent and sad, behind the net curtain of the kitchen window, his wife was watching him as intently as he himself was gazing after Webber.

Webber was all right, Burnstead though. Well, he was all right as long as he stuck to gardening and forgot that he'd been a policeman. A bit of an old meddler. You had to be polite of course, certainly you did; that only made sense, that did. Unless he was going to stir things up and turn everything into a Godawful mess. The less Mr. Clever Webber knew, the better. Not all his fault—the Thomas woman didn't help; she was a real pusher. Women; women were a right bloody nuisance.

As he continued his leisurely walk alone, Webber envied him. He didn't envy Ted Snow with his grand office in Scotland Yard, but Burnstead's life of gentle detection in his own village seemed to Webber to be very near to perfection—a silly envy, he told himself, as he skirted the north wall of the churchyard, for, at the moment at least, that seemed to be exactly what he had for himself. He paused to note with interest that neither the children nor Joan Coley were interrupting Harry Fellows at his work. If anyone, it was the vicar himself who was delaying progress and engaging his lame duck in earnest conversation. Really, Webber thought, you didn't need to hear what Coley was saying, he was a man who relied on dumbshow as much as the spoken word. He wore his habitual grey suit of battered and shapeless tweed and, unsuitably for the muddy churchyard, a pair of tartan carpet slippers. His arms described vast rolling gestures as if gathering up great mounds of earth and then depositing them delicately in descending undulations like some manic Capability Brown. The wings of his white hair flew with enthusiasm and his eyes bulged with fervour.

"Mad as a hatter," said Joan Coley, who had arrived unnoticed at Webber's side.

"What exactly is the general plan?" he asked with interest.

"Tidying up." Joan sighed resignedly. "Although goodness knows why William bothers. It's the oldest part of the churchyard and so tucked away that it seems a waste of effort. Anyway, I rather liked it as it was, jammed full and not looking much different from the common, apart from all the headstones, of course."

"They won't move those?"

"Gracious no, that would literally mean moving heaven and earth as well as the Archdeacon and probably having to have tea with his awful wife—oh dear, aren't I naughty? I'm not really disloyal you know," she reproved Webber as he grinned broadly, "only sometimes I do find the parish a bit of a strain."

" 'Mad as a hatter' is a bit strong perhaps," Webber said.

"Not really," Joan said comfortably. "No, I don't call that disloyal. William knows quite well that I say that. No, I suppose it's a question of priorities. I mean, I ask you, he's got two parishes—there's St. Paul's at Lower Henworth as well as St. Peter's here—and I suppose he's lucky with a regular congregation in either of them of—what, fifteen? We are so lucky with our churches. The most beautiful in the world, William says, here in Suffolk. But then what good is that if people won't come?"

Webber thought of Coley's earnest but confused sermons but was too nice to refer to them. Instead he said, "Getting the message across instead of making sure the roof doesn't fall in, you mean?"

"Yes, that is just what I do mean, I suppose, but of course I wouldn't ever say so. Poor dear, now that would be really disloyal and William is really such a good man, you know. I always think Christianity is so difficult if you're quite sane. Which reminds me that I must write to that poor Ruth Greenwood. We had such a nice letter from her. I expect you've heard that her mother is almost quite well again? Such a blessing. Ruth was asking about her little cottage and of course she's paid her rent in advance so it's quite safe and waiting for her. She seems to have taken a liking to Flaxfield and it must have painful memories for her down here. Aren't people odd?''

''Very,'' Webber said.

'' 'Let me now go into the field and glean among the ears of corn,' '' Joan quoted vaguely. ''William will see she comes to no harm, I'm sure; he will keep an eye on her. William takes care of everyone. Stupid man, he'll get his feet so wet in those slippers. I think I ought to take him some hot coffee.''

When at last she arrived with two cups of coffee, both Webber and her husband had gone. Oh well, it would be a pity to waste it, or the excuse to stay and drink it with Harry herself. She picked her way through the overgrown grass towards him, where he stood leaning dejectedly on the handle of a shovel and deep in thought. She hoped William wasn't overworking him. Harry was big and strong but sometimes, she thought, not as young as he looked. Once, she had asked William his age but he had changed the subject as he so often did where Harry was concerned. She knew less about Harry, she realised, than anyone else in the village. There was rumour and gossip, of course, but they were deadlier sins, she knew in Williams's eyes, than the other seven put together. He didn't mean it, but sometimes life with William could be very lonely.

''Rushed off somewhere, has he? Oh dear, what a husband! Is he coming back or shall I join you? I'm certainly not wasting good coffee.''

Harry took the tray from her and placed it on the flat grave of Tabitha Meadows, who had rested in peace since 1780. He recognised the forced jolly tone that she nearly always used when they were alone. He didn't mind it; he liked to see her saying one thing while she was thinking something different. But he was always careful not to be too jolly with her. Respect, that was the tack with Mrs. Coley. One day he might need her help and she would remember his respect.

"Vicar's gone off to look at the font. He's talkin' of moving it again." He allowed himself a rueful sigh. "Heavy old thing that is, too."

"Oh really! Isn't he the limit? It's been perfectly happy where you moved it for safety under the tower ever since the builders were repairing the roof of the nave. Do drink this while it's still lukewarm. Don't you worry, Harry, I'll have a word with him." She laughed almost girlishly. "I think I can change his mind. I should be able to after all these years."

"I wouldn't like Mr. Coley to think I'm complaining."

"Of course not, I promise he won't think that. Sometimes I think he takes advantage of you."

Ruth had not waited for a reply to her letter and came back to her cottage later that afternoon. She felt guilty about leaving her mother, but not much. There was Auntie Rose and the shop—between them they would stimulate her recovery. I am where I should be, she thought; it was a duty she owed Joseph as well as to herself and it was right that she should have returned, and alone, like a cat with buttered paws. She made herself some tea and drank it without any real pleasure, trying to convince herself that she had done the sensible thing. She had left the cottage in a mess but now it was clean and tidy. That would be Mrs. Thomas. Well, you couldn't hardly resent kindness, although, of course, she did and for a moment she pictured herself traveling eternally between London and Flaxfield bouncing from her mother to Mrs. Thomas and back like a manic ballbearing on a pin table. She wondered how long it would be before her car attracted the attention of either John Webber or his Welsh friend. She left the tea unfinished and drove off in the car without stopping to think where she was going, only just now, she didn't want to talk to either of them. It did not surprise her that the car drove itself to Wangford without any conscious effort on her part. She had driven to Warren Lane before and had stopped and stared at Fox House. Now she didn't give it a glance because she hoped she might see Harry's motorbike. She knew that he lived somewhere near Victoria Varley's house because he'd told her, and it was Harry who filled the whole of her mind and only Harry who had made her come back to Flaxfield. Nothing to do with Joseph or the money any more, not remotely. It was Harry, the one they talked and gossiped about in the shops and the pub because he had made love to a woman who was on television, who was old enough to be his mother.

There were not many houses, one or two cottages in the gaps between the high hedgerows and the steep banks with wild flowers she didn't know the names of, only that they were simple and beautiful and unspoilt, like Harry. He was more than that, though: a mixture of sadness and shyness until, when you made him forget that he was a labourer covered in mud, he let you know that he had a good mind and could make you laugh. She thought of him in a suit playing bridge with her mother and Auntie Rose. She thought of him with no suit and no clothes at all.

He did have some clothes on, only a pair of old grey flannel trousers, and he was doing something to the motorbike parked on the patch of front garden, even smaller than her own in Flaxfield, the one he had offered to dig for her.

"Hullo then! You lookin' for me or just passing?"

Well thank God you couldn't be more natural or honest than that. It would make a change for them in the shops and the pub, something new for them.

"Looking for you. I wondered if you'd like to have a meal with me tonight. Not in Flaxfield. Some where nice and quiet. I wondered if you knew anywhere?"

FIFTEEN

Webber was not a man given to hasty judgements and it was not in his nature to jump to conclusions, yet as the days went by and the evenings grew longer he began to wonder if he had done just that. But deep within him he did not believe it. There were too many things that didn't add up. He smiled ruefully at himself; maths had never been his strongest subject.

"I shouldn't worry about that," Mrs. Thomas told him cheerfully on the bowling green behind The Bull. "Anyone can press buttons on a pocket calculator"—she took elaborate aim with her wood—"it's people, not numbers, you're good at."

Webber followed the speeding wood and watched it thump into the ditch and over the bank of retaining turf. "It's not ninepins, Lizzie, you know; the idea is to sneak up gently on the jack and surprise it." Winning made him feel better and they joined Betsey and Doreen at a rickety table under a tree.

"You're supposed to walk gently after the ball," Betsey reproved her, "not try and race it."

"And you didn't misunderstand her about her feelings for Harry Fellows?" Webber asked him, taking up the conversation when the game had interrupted it. "I mean, she wasn't implying that it was just a casual affair?"

Betsey shook his head and thought carefully to remember her words. "No, she did say that at first . . . she thought it was only sex, but then she found that she'd done a stupid thing and fallen in love with him."

"If she thought it was stupid," Webber said, after a long pull at his beer, "perhaps she wanted to get away from him."

"I don't think she meant that kind of stupid. I think she meant stupid because she couldn't do anything about it. I felt sorry for her."

"Not a nice woman," Doreen said primly. "Carrying on with a man not much more than a boy. If something has happened to her it wouldn't surprise me."

"Is that what people are saying?" Webber asked mildly.

"You must have heard the rumours," Doreen said. "They're saying she's dead."

"And do they say who did it?" Webber didn't look directly at Dorcen but fished in his pocket for his pipe and tobacco. "Young Harry, I suppose?"

"A lover's quarrel seems the most popular," Betsey said. "Why not someone who was jealous of them? He's a nice looking chap. I should think Victoria wasn't the only one to set her heart on him. Anyway, that's all it amounts to—idle, vicious gossip from people with nothing better to do."

Mrs. Thomas noted with interest that her daughter was flushing with anger, although it was plain to her that Betsey hadn't meant it as a personal attack on his wife. He was himself quite pink, she noticed, but that, she guessed, was a combination of indignation and because he was a nice sentimental creature who disliked revealing his personal affections in public.

"Well, you could say that they were an oddly matched pair," Webber said, "but I've known stranger couplings."

"If anyone has a right to say that they're worried about her, then he has," Betsey said.

"And does he?"

"Yes, he does. He's reported her as missing to the police, but Sergeant Burnstead doesn't seem to take it very seriously. He just teased Harry, said that he had a lot to learn about women."

"A subject the sergeant is well versed in," Doreen sniffed.

There was a silence while they all remembered the complexities of Constable Burnstead's amorous village peccadillos before being elevated to the sober status of sergeant.

"You haven't told us what you think, John," Betsey said at last.

"Burnstead is a good copper," Webber said. "If I were in his place, I'd probably be saying much the same thing."

And that, thought Mrs. Thomas with satisfaction, is as much as you'll get out of him, and quite right, too. She was relieved to learn that, so far, Ruth's confidence about the missing money had not leaked out to the village.

The shadows of the last few players on the green stretched long over the turf, caught sharp by the last rays of the sun sneaking through the branches of the trees.

Flaxfield residents were used to summer tourists. They came in organised coaches from London and at lunchtime they could often be seen in The Bull seeking sustenance between churches. It was unusual to see them in the evening and when April Schittski and Benjamin emerged from the saloon bar carrying drinks their presence did not go unnoticed.

"Americans," Doreen said unnecessarily. It was not a difficult identification since Benjamin had insisted on them dressing the part and they could hardly have been taken for anything else.

"Perhaps they've missed their coach," Betsey said. "It's happened before."

Webber watched them with interest, as they drifted round

the green, edging their way past the locals like gaudy tropical fish in a tankful of brown trout.

"They're not in a coach party," Mrs. Thomas said authoritatively. "I happened to see her in the Co-op this morning. She was having difficulty trying to buy crackers and candy. She's a Mrs. Lamb, comes from Dallas, her husband is a doctor, and they've rented one of Mr. Gough's holiday houses. I don't know what they're paying for it yet," she concluded apologetically.

As if to confirm the accuracy of her intelligence, Mr. Gough himself joined his clients carrying a plateful of inelegant sandwiches.

"She has a good appetite," Webber said. He liked to see people enjoying their food. "Anything else?"

"They're looking for antiques to furnish their house. I got the impression it was a second home, but I didn't like to pry."

"Of course not. Ah, Vicar! Good evening, and Mrs. Coley, too. Won't you join us? The tables seem rather full tonight—the usual crush before they call last orders. Taking a little fuel for the spirit before the rigours of the weekend?"

"Joan dear, how nice," Betsey said with genuine pleasure. "Come and sit next to me. How smart you look." He believed in complimenting her even though tonight, he thought, she looked like a battered moth.

"I'd like to believe you," Joan said, "but you mustn't make it so difficult for me. Perhaps it was smart once. I think it's what used to be called a tea gown. At least the material is good—that is probably why it's lasted so long."

"You look very nice," Betsey said loyally. He followed Joan's squinting gaze across the darkening bowling green to where April sat. Her dress was a blaze of colour in a spotlight of the setting sun. "I hope you're not being seduced by transatlantic fashion,'' he said with mock severity. ''Those colours should be strictly reserved for stained glass windows.''

''We were talking to them at the bar for a moment,'' Joan said, ''before Mr. Gough whisked them away. He seemed very solicitous so I imagine they must be very wealthy. I thought they seemed rather nice.''

''I'm sure they are,'' Coley said. ''I suppose one mustn't blame them for wanting to buy antiques. After all, why not, if they have the money? It seems sad in one way, things leaving the country, but they are only things. People are so much more important.''

''And they've come such a long way,'' Joan said vaguely. ''At least, I suppose Dallas is a long way. It's in the middle somewhere, isn't it?''

''It seems almost frighteningly near when you see it on television,'' Coley said. ''It is odd that they should want to make programmes like that, isn't it? I mean it shows everyone in such a bad light, all that obsession with money and material things, surely it's not the kind of image they wish to project, not seriously.''

''I don't think you are meant to take it seriously,'' Webber said. ''You mustn't judge people by the films they make, Vicar, or we should all look very odd in England.''

''You are all very odd in England,'' Mrs. Thomas said. ''In Suffolk, anyway.''

''Certainly I think we are just as obsessed with money,'' Joan said. ''More perhaps, because we haven't got very much. Just think how ghastly *we* must have been when we were rich and doing the Grand Tour all over Europe.''

''I don't think Americans are ghastly,'' Betsey said, ''and I love 'Dallas.' It's a fairy story—all those frocks and the make-up. I'm mad about it. You're not meant to believe it, only enjoy it. I wonder where they find girls with their eyes so far apart?''

"I expect there's an operation," Doreen said, "like they do noses."

"I must admit that I do find difficulty with the language," Coley said. "She told me that she likes Flaxfield, she thinks it's more than beautiful. It's cute, she said, a truly meaningful experience. She and her husband are seriously trying to reestablish their priorities."

For several quite different reasons the company regarded the Americans with interest until all their glasses were empty.

"Such a perfect evening," Coley said sadly, as they strolled homewards together. "However, all good things. . . ."

The little party paused outside Trottwood Antiques where, on a sudden impulse, Mrs. Thomas drew her daughter on one side while the others were saying a reluctant goodnight on the first really warm summer night of the year.

"Supper? How wonderful, what a lovely idea," Joan said impulsively, "but really we couldn't. I mean, at such short notice—no honestly!"

"You needn't worry about that," Doreen said. "Mam will cope with everything, she always does."

"Please!" Betsey pleaded. "Unplanned parties are always the best, unless you have anything spoiling in the oven of course." It was a kind proviso and he felt quite safe in making it.

Joan wondered if she could make bread and cheese sound interesting but gratefully abandoned the effort. "Well no, not really. Something quite simple. Cold, actually. Shopping is such a problem, isn't it? William has been working on his sermon and by the time I'd finished the ladies flower rota— Oh golly! A walled garden. I had no idea you had such a lovely corner tucked away at the back here. Honeysuckle and a rambling rose! I can't bear it!"

"I thought we could eat out here," Betsey said happily.

"The table will be plenty big enough. It came from a farm kitchen and I couldn't bring myself to sell it. John, come and help me with some chairs. And we shall have Chianti," he sang happily to himself, doing a little dance as he left them.

There was Chianti, bottles of Chianti, with the table glowing in the light of the Victorian oil lamps Doreen brought out from the shop while her mother made enough spaghetti to feed them all generously, steaming with garlic and green olive oil with a pound of crisp bacon crumbled into it for good measure.

"Quite perfect." Coley beamed at Betsey, who was in the corner where he was adjusting the portable tape recorder to play softly. "It should only be Delius tonight, and if by any chance it happens to be Vaughan Williams then please don't tell me. I intend to enjoy it as Delius, and then it will be."

In the idle discussion that followed, Joan caught Doreen's eye and, mellow with wine and music, whispered happily, "Isn't your mother a wonderful cook?"

"Wonderful," Doreen agreed. "Sometimes I could hit her."

"I had toyed with the idea of the story Ruth for my sermon," Coley was saying, "but it all got rather complicated, I'm afraid, so I have fallen back on one of my old standbys. Unenterprising, I dare say, but I suppose no one will care very much. I wonder if our friend Gough will steer his rich clients your way, Trottwood?" He had never quite brought himself to call him Betsey.

"I doubt it," Betsey said. "At least, I sincerely hope not. I never want to sell anything I really like. I'm quite happy passing on a few pot lids or horse brasses."

"What a very lucky man you are," Coley said without envy, "surrounded by things you enjoy so much and not having to sell them."

With the opening of the last bottle of wine, and while

Doreen and Mrs. Thomas were serving the coffee, Betsey quietly brought out the old man's copy of the Spencer painting and propped it against the back of a chair, so that it sat with a background of Russian Vine, bathed in the mellow light from the oil lamps.

Gradually the company fell silent, so that there was only the music and the painting.

"I see what you mean," Coley said at last. "In this sort of light you could, indeed, be looking at a genuine masterpiece by Stanley Spencer."

He was right, Mrs. Thomas thought, the painting did indeed look very like the Spencer paintings she had seen in the Tate Gallery.

"Did you ever find out anything about the ship?" Webber asked.

"It seems it never existed," Betsey said. "At least, there's no record of such a name at Lloyd's."

"No, no, of course not," Coley said in mild astonishment. "Forgive me, I thought it was rather obvious."

SIXTEEN

"All my life," Webber said, gazing gloomily at the painting, "I have been missing the obvious. It's an occupational hazard for a policeman. I find it with crosswords, too. I stare at the clue and it stares back at me. Usually, I regret to say, Mrs. Thomas will break off from her labours and tell me the answer, to which I always say 'Yes, of course' and to which she invariably replies 'No, not "Of course"—"Clever Lizzie." ' I hope I can trust you to spare us that, Vicar?"

Red wine was inclined to bring out one of Webber's pompous passages. Mrs. Thomas hoped that it wouldn't develop into a sneezing fit, which it sometimes did.

"It isn't really clever," Coley said. "I suppose you could say that I had a head start. Indeed, it would have been very odd if I had missed it. The painting doesn't concern the ship, does it? It is the men on the beach who must have been the focus for the artist, surely?"

"The fishermen and the foreman," Betsey said, staring at the man with the outstretched arm and the glaring eyes, "and it must be the beach at Dunwold."

"Dunwold may well have been the inspiration but it's the Sea of Galilee," Coley said. "The fishermen are Simon called Peter and his brother Andrew. The foreman is of course Jesus. 'Follow me and I will make you fishers of men.' "

"St. Matthew," Joan said dutifully.

"Matthew, chapter four, verse nineteen," Coley said. "You see? 'Mat. IV. 19,' not 'Mativig.' "

"Of course!" Webber said instinctively.

"No—'Clever William,' " Joan said and refilled all the glasses in a burst of loyal enthusiasm while studiously avoiding Doreen's warning glance.

"So it wasn't a title, it was part of a signature," Betsey said. "The original was probably signed down in the corner somewhere. The 'SS' is for 'Stanley Spencer.' The old man probably didn't think it looked important enough there for a title. What a pity we can't have a Resurrection at St.Peter's. Mrs. Teasdale's father might tell us where to find the original he copied it from."

Coley nodded sadly. " 'The Resurrection at Cookham.' The church there is very lucky—they have his 'Last Supper.'

I believe they've had to enlarge the car park to accommodate all the tourist coaches. Just think of it—'The Flaxfield Spencer'! How wonderful."

"When did Spencer come to Wangford?" Webber asked.

"A long time ago," Betsey said. "He married his first wife there. I know they had their honeymoon round here, and went down to the coast. He must have painted it then, when he was happy. Goodness knows when Mrs. Teasdale's father, old Abner Gosse, saw it. He must have seen the original, I can't find any record of it being reproduced as I thought once. It's probably disappeared years ago."

"Spencer came back on his own," Coley said, "after the divorce. His second wife was not a nice woman, I'm afraid. Poor Spencer—a most complicated simple man. I should dearly like to have talked to him."

Webber remembered Joan Coley saying, "William takes care of everyone." There was no doubting his sincerity, Webber reflected, but even well intentioned meddling was not a virtue he admired.

"Take it," Betsey said suddenly, "take it and have it in St. Peter's. Have it as an altar-piece, why not? Nice dim light and at a distance you've got our masterpiece."

"I think it's time to cork up the wine," Doreen said.

"I mean it," Betsey said, glowing with generosity and Co-op Chianti.

"Wouldn't you have to get permission from the Archdeacon?" Joan asked apprehensively.

"Not at all," Coley said, already standing proprietorily in front of the painting with his hands clasped behind his back. "One could hardly describe the acquisition of a painting as a structural alteration. That, of course, would require archidiaconal permission."

"My dear," Joan said, "I hardly think . . . Well, after all, it is only a copy."

Coley detached his hands but kept his eyes on the picture. His arms described a gentle circular motion before it as though willing them to translate his thoughts into words.

He is like a child, Betsey thought, like a child imagining his toy pedal car is a space rocket flying to the moon. Like an alchemist turning base metal into gold or Vaughan Williams into Delius.

"I think," Doreen said, rising unsteadily, "that we should all sleep on it before we make any hasty decisions. It may only be a copy but it was quite an expensive outlay for us."

Far from disconcerting Coley, her words seemed to synchronise his arms and thoughts. "How much?" he said almost fiercely.

"Nothing," Betsey said, ignoring Doreen. "It's a gift. I don't advise you to carry it back tonight. It's bound to cause comment. People will think you've been robbing the shop. I'll deliver it for you, all part of the service."

"Leave the washing up," Mrs. Thomas said to Doreen as they were all saying their separate goodnights. "I'll come round in the morning. With any luck we'll have a storm in the night and that will do most of it for us." In an unusual display of maternal affection she kissed her daughter on the cheek. "Best leave it. You're right—sleep on it."

"I'm damned if I'll put anything in his rotten old collection bag ever again."

"You're thinking of chapel in Wales when you were a little girl."

"I'm not joking."

"Oh I know that. You never did joke about money. Well, you'll be able to think of the painting as a season ticket, won't you? John, are you walking me home or not?"

Joan Coley had dozed off in her chair with a smile of grateful repletion. In a corner of the garden Webber took his leave of a flushed and gesticulating Coley.

"Getting excited about his new altar-piece, was he?" Mrs. Thomas asked Webber, as they strolled in the cool breeze of the High Street.

"I was asking him why anyone should think Harry Fellows was a lame duck. He didn't tell me."

"Didn't or wouldn't?"

"It was rather like one of his sermons—it takes him a long time to say nothing. Coley's a bit of a fool, but luckily he's an honest fool, otherwise he would simply have said that he didn't know. Here we are, safe and sound. Would a night-cap be a good idea?"

At the back of her mind she knew she had something she wanted to tell him but the Chianti on top of the Guinness at the pub defeated her. "It would be, if we hadn't had more than enough already. Besides, that evil face at the window means I've got a starving cat waiting for me. Give us a kiss nice and tidy. There's always tomorrow."

Not always, he thought, not for everyone, but he was glad that he hadn't said it.

On the mat she found a letter from Andy Baldwin, the young policeman she had first met in Ruth Greenwood's gallery. It was not the first time he had written. She fed the indignant and importunate Bunter before reading it and then, even though she was tired and longed for her bed, she sat down at the kitchen table and answered it as carefully and honestly as she had answered all his other letters.

In the morning Harry appeared at Trottwood Antiques early to collect the painting. It was early because it had occurred to Coley that in the sober light of the morning Betsey could change his mind. The shop was open but empty and Harry found Doreen in the walled garden staring disconsolately at the debris of the night before. There had been no convenient rainstorm in the night.

"It's packed and ready for you. Mr. Trottwood would have delivered it himself later," she said coldly, hoping that some of her obvious displeasure would be conveyed to the wretched vicar with whom she was out of sympathy. A glance at Harry's open and smiling face convinced her that it was to be a hope unfulfilled.

"And I was to tell you special," he said, "that they both enjoyed themselves very much and they'll be writin' to thank you properly." He smiled around at the plates of congealed spaghetti with interest.

It was curious, she thought. Although he always conveyed an impression of quiet reserve, even shyness, beneath that she sensed something quite at odds with it. It was something she found difficult to name. Arrogance and menace were too strong, but Doreen had known many men before Betsey had lulled her into the gentle acceptance of man's better nature and she was surprised to be reminded of her early adventures when danger signals had flown with exciting frequency. It seemed a long time ago.

"Bit of a party was it? Mr. Trottwood sleeping it off?"

"He's gone up to London on business." She had meant it to sound reproving, not inviting, and qualified it severely. "I should think he was up long before you were."

Harry nodded amiably. "Shouldn't wonder. Don't like getting up early. I've had enough of that."

That would be when he was in the orphanage, Doreen thought. She was well up on local gossip in general and on Harry in particular. It had intrigued her that her mother had never speculated about Harry or the rumours circulating around him and, for Doreen, that made him even more interesting. She wished that she had put on something more attractive than an old skirt and jumper, but she had dressed for washing-up.

"I'll give you a hand," he said, as though he had read her

mind. "They'll need soaking," he said in the kitchen. "Quicker in the end. Give them half-an-hour in the hot water first. Anything else I can give you a hand with?"

She saw herself so clearly uttering a terse refusal of any further help and opening the kitchen door for him with brusque thanks, that it came as a shock to find herself still sharing the towel to dry their hands, and to hear herself saying that she ought to be making the bed.

Benjamin Lamb was wet and unhappy and April was equally miserable. For days they had allowed Mr. Gough to drive them around the countryside visiting antique shops, both humble and grand. In all of them it was obvious to Benjamin that prices had been suitably adjusted. Forewarned by Gough, the owners had dutifully inflated their prices so that Gough could be paid his commission. It hadn't bothered Benjamin, who had no intention of buying anything. Some of the things they had seen had been good but nothing that he wanted to buy for the kind of clients he had in mind. He had cautiously let it be known that he was only interested in something quite exceptional and outstanding. Modern English paintings were his great enthusiasm, he told everyone. Not just ordinary paintings. Hockney or Spencer, that sort of thing.

Wherever Joseph had seen it, then it most certainly hadn't been in a shop. He had accepted Gough's offer only after visiting the village of Wangford himself and being bitterly disappointed. Wangford could hardly lay claim to being one of the great antique centres of England or even of Suffolk, and now after the last abortive foray into the farthest outskirts of the surrounding towns and villages, he and April stood miserably in the soaking wet courtyard of Gough's Flaxfield sale-room while waiting for him to put the car away and open it up for them.

"I want to go home," April said, as Gough hopped his

way towards them over the puddles flurried with driving rain, "and I don't mean that crummy dump this oily old bastard calls a house. I mean home to civilization."

"Shut up," Benjamin said softly but with deep feeling. "For God's sake go and find someone to play with."

The store-room of Gough and Groucher's sale-room had been converted from an old barn in the days of Mr. Gough's grandfather. The roof leaked when it rained heavily, as it was raining now. The water dripped onto a motley collection of household goods ranging from undistinguished furniture to a pathetic collection of personal effects. Tea caddies and clocks, which had once been joined in the happy ceremony of a thousand tea-times, lay silent and sad among the snap-shot albums with the sepia faces of the families who would never again say "Ah! That was good, I was just ready for that!"

"Dross," Mr. Gough said pontifically. "Not at all typical of our usual sales as I told you. Sadly, you happen to have missed some of our best collections earlier in the year. However, one never knows. . . . There's a particularly fine set of very old Toby Jugs down here somewhere. Now they would certainly grace a kitchen dresser. Excuse me a moment, Mrs. Lamb. Just browse around and I'll go and see if I can find them."

He left April standing in disbelief at an ancient electric fire with lumps of coloured glass piled up in front, presumably to immitate a blazing coal fire. She felt very sorry for herself. Ben had often been rude and unkind to her—she should be used to it by now—but rudeness on top of pouring rain in this awful dump they called a village was too much.

Benjamin ignored the Toby Jugs and was on his hands and knees before the piled canvases of Abner Gosse.

Gough said, "Yes, now those really are quite interesting. I was going to draw your attention to them. Painted by one of our local celebrities. He died quite recently, completely untutored, of course, but a natural primitive talent, don't you think? Cleaned up and properly framed? The naïveté of Grandma Moses coupled with''—Mr. Gough searched his mind desperately and prayed that the name of that painter he had recently seen reproduced with such ghastly clarity in a Sunday colour magazine would come and complete his essay into the contemporary American art scene—''coupled with the exciting plagiarism of Andy Warhol.'' He concluded with relief and considerable satisfaction that, not only the wretched man's name, but the headline of the article, had so providentially floated into his head. ''Exciting plagiarism'' could just as well serve for Abner Gosse as the Warhol man; after all, tins of tomato soup and Coca-Cola bottles were surely no more original than the old man's careful copies of the Guinness Toucan or a Rolls-Royce amid the ruins of ancient Greece.

Benjamin crouched on his toes and sorted through the paintings one by one. Like all dealers, except when they are selling, he was not given to enthusiasm and he certainly had no intention of praising an auctioneer's goods to his face. All the same, whether by luck or genuine insight, there was something in what Gough had said. The paintings did have a kind of primitive charm. No, they had something more than that, even though some of them were painted on scraps of paper stuck onto cardboard—the artist had not believed in wasting money on canvas or frames. In his mind's eye he saw them expensively displayed and catalogued in a special New York exhibition. If he was not going to find a masterpiece by Stanley Spencer then he might do worse than to promote an unknown English primitive of genius—well, he would tell them he was a genius.

''Amusing,'' he said dismissively, ''but you won't break

any records, I'm afraid. Is this the lot or are there any more lying around?''

''I believe there is another one knocking about somewhere,'' Gough said stiffly. ''His daughter sold one locally, I believe.''

Mrs. Thomas and Webber sat on the wooden seat in the wilderness of her garden digesting their evening meal with a glass of red wine.

''A great improvement on Betsey's Chianti,'' he said happily.

''He never had a good mouth for wine, I'm afraid.'' The frown of concentration cleared from her face. ''I knew there was something I couldn't remember the other night. You know I told you that I'd translated for that Mrs. Lamb in the Co-op?''

''Yes, she was asking for crackers and something else, wasn't she?''

''Candy. She wanted to know if they sold Hershey bars.''

SEVENTEEN

April had no intention of finding someone to play with when she left the sale-room to walk back to the house alone. She was homesick and miserable. Ben could make you feel like losing a set-point on a double fault and then losing the match itself. But Ben was where the money was and she knew it, whatever else he was, he wasn't mean. There was always plenty of cash, and like Joseph Greenwood he believed in using it like a weapon; cash was power and you didn't walk out on power. It was better than love. Love was for kids in Ohio. Even the occasional sex with Ben had long since become no more than a loveless relief, as much, she suspected, for him as for her.

She slouched unhappily some way along the wet road before remembering that she had left her raincoat in Gough's car. She was certainly not going back for it; she could change when she got back. Near the church the rain turned into a hissing downpour with a flash of lightning and thunder so close upon it that it sounded like the crack of a gun above her head. St. Peter's was the nearest shelter and she ran into it for sanctuary from the storm.

It took her some moments to adjust to the gloom. There were lights down at the end near the altar where some men seemed to be working but most of the church was as dark as the sky outside, until the lightning blazed through the coloured glass windows brighter than sudden sunlight. It should have been the painting hanging in glory that first caught her eye, but it was Harry Fellows helping the vicar to hang the painting over the altar who riveted her attention.

"Up a bit on your left," the old man with the wild hair was saying.

The altar had been decently covered with a dust sheet to protect it from the step-ladder on the very top of which stood a young man in jeans and a white tee shirt. The ladder was barely high enough and he pushed himself up on his toes, his extended arms strained sideways from his body as he reached agonisingly to adjust the links in the chain he was holding in each hand, slipping them on and off the nails in the beam above him. The chains supported the painting over the altar below.

In the dramatic light of the storm he looked like a grotesque tableau vivant of the Crucifixion.

Soaked with rain, she sat at the back of the church in the shadow of the great Perpendicular font with its spiked, pinnacled cover of carved wood. Her eyes couldn't leave the straining figure and she only half heard the older man's commands like some manic husband teaching his wife how to park the car.

"Right hand down a bit—and steady! There! Hold it."

When at last he was satisfied and had admired the painting long enough, they restored the altar to sanctity and the instructor disappeared.

April hoped that the young man wouldn't follow him and he didn't.

He had watched her from the height of the step-ladder. From there it had seemed that she was wearing a very tight dress but now, as he strolled towards her with his coat flung over his shoulder, he could see that her clothes were wet and clinging to her. Like that girl in the book he'd read; she had been wet and alone in a church, too; he'd forgotten why but it didn't matter. That woman wrote good books. Barbara something. She knew about girls and about men, too, and money. Yes, really good. He'd get another when the library van came round next time. What had that girl been doing in that church? Yes, of course, she'd come to pray to get her voice back, after she'd been frightened by a burglar. And then in the church this shy young farmer had spoken to her.

Harry grinned shyly at April. "You're sopping wet. You won't 'arf cop it if those old flower biddies catch you dripping all over their pews."

"You wanna know something?" April said seriously. "I've been told to find someone to play with."

It was ten days later when Webber telephoned Ted Snow's

home and spoke to his wife, Betty. If he could help it, Webber never phoned Ted at his office. There were people at the Yard who disapproved of their friendship and of Superintendant Snow's belief that such a friendship deserved more than the casual exchange of Christmas cards.

"At least golf widows get to see their husbands at night," Betty said. "I haven't seen Ted for five weeks, not even an odd Sunday. We talk on the phone but that's about it. I spoke to him last night and there's a message for you, by the way, so I'm glad you called."

"I rather hoped there might be."

"It's not much. You know he doesn't like saying much on the phone. I'm to tell you that he's heard from America. Make sense?"

"When do you think he might be back?"

"Quite soon, I hope. He's down in darkest Wales, somewhere called Llanwinny. A farmer murdered his wife—at least, everyone down there seems to think so."

"And Ted?"

"Oh yes, he thinks so, too. Not easy to prove apparently, that's why he's taking so long over it—there's no body."

"Snap."

"You, too?"

"I think so. Poor Ted—I know how he feels. Bodies are always such a comfort. Oh well, at least I can sleep in my own bed."

"How is Lizzie?" Betty's questions were never subtle.

"A bit of a handful and the joy of my life, only don't tell her."

"Why not? I like to hear it. We hoped you might be married by now."

"We manage well enough."

"Dear John, it is nice to hear you. You'll come and see us? I'll ring you when he's back."

"Hardly the right moment to welcome the hunter home from the hills. You'll want to be alone."

"How nice to be treated like a young bride again. It's our silver wedding soon. Don't be daft, we shall love to have you and you'll be able to talk properly—cheer each other up. Will you bring Lizzie? You'll have to share a bedroom, I'm afraid."

Webber grinned without letting it creep into his voice. "It depends what she's up to, but yes, certainly. I'd love to come up for a night. Save me the drive back on the same day."

"Poor old man, you do love to play the ancient, don't you? Do try and bring Lizzie, then at least we'll have a decent meal. Oh dear, what a selfish invitation. Don't tell her that, just say we'd love to see her."

"I'll tell her, I promise, but you know Lizzie, she may have other fish to fry."

"The nineteenth verse—of the fourth chapter—of the gospel according to St. Matthew," the Reverend William Coley intoned earnestly and waited for the congregation to compose itself. " 'Follow me'!" Coley shouted suddenly, like a Commando sergeant rallying his troops. The platoon in the pews jumped impressively and subsided into respectful silence.

" 'Follow me,' " Coley repeated, slowly and conspiratorially, " 'and I will make you fishers of men.' "

You could hardly say that the village was out in force, Betsey thought from his vantage pew at the back of the nave, but it was certainly a better turnout than usual. Word of the vicar's acquisition had permeated Flaxfield and stimulated curiosity. It was a pity that there couldn't have been a modestly printed acknowledgement somewhere: "Altar-piece kindly donated by Trottwood Antiques." Perhaps that was expecting too much and Coley himself had somewhat disappointingly described it merely as "A superb example of local primitive art'' and passed on to the theme of the painting and the message of his sermon.

Joan Coley composed her features dutifully into pious attention and considered the possibilities for Sunday lunch. New sermons were always a hazard. It was probably best to plan something simple: there was that splendid tin of ham from her sister's Christmas hamper, of course, but without the comfort of it on the larder shelf she would feel naked. Suppose someone got married. A vicar's wife should always be able to command ham sandwiches. Perhaps Harry would marry someone and settle down. She didn't wish Victoria Varley any harm, but really, it was a blessing that she had gone away. Marriage should surely be with someone nearer his own age.

She regretted her ordained position of privilege so near to William and the pulpit. Quite apart from giving her a stiff neck every Sunday, she could not easily see just who was sitting behind her. Earlier she had been surprised to see Harry dressed respectably in his Sunday best. Surprised because Harry was not a churchgoer. She supposed that he had succumbed to William's enthusiasm and come to see the painting that together they had hung so carefully over the altar. William's enthusiasm; well, that had always been a problem. Less now, mercifully, when it could be channelled into sensible energy-consuming efforts, like saving the church roof or the timbers of the bell tower, and with luck the new altarpiece should literally prove a blessing and an inspiration for many sermons to come. At least you could sit through a sermon in comparative comfort. She thought back to the early years when William had taken her many miles on forced marches protesting against nuclear war, and even before that the long, rain-soaked vigils outside prisons in the days when they still hanged people for murder. There had been some who had called him a saint then. Some, but not many.

"And straightway," William's finger pointed at the painting dramatically, "no excuses, no dithering, not 'Just let us tidy up the nets first,' but straightway, immediately, they walked away from everything they owned in the world and followed him."

Mrs. Fronefield sat with Ruth and gave William her full attention, or as much of it as a busy mind would allow. You could leave a business when a daughter needed you but surely to abandon an abundant harvest of fish at the casual command of a total stranger came perilously close to irresponsibility. You didn't get a Queen's Award for Industry by letting your assets rot on the beach, although, of course, the Queen was the head of the Church of England, not that *she* would have believed all this either. Surely she was too bright to believe in such fairy stories? Any more than Lionel had, any more than Ruth did. Ruth—a good daughter, but a worry. "Mummy you'd better come down here and stay with me for a while. To hell with the shop and with Auntie Rose, you've had a shock, you need peace and quiet." A daughter called and you came. Ruth could give what reasons she liked but she needed her mother and in her own stubborn time she would tell her why, not that a mother couldn't guess already. The girl was in love, that's what she was. No wonder she had chosen to stay down here. Joseph's money she'd never find again, that was not the reason. The reason was sitting only a few feet on front of them in a terrible suit with only twenty per cent wool in it—if that, and Ruth couldn't take her eyes off him. All right, so shoulders like a navvy and a face like a sexy schoolboy and Ruth far too ready with his name, and she should leave a good business and follow rubbish like that? Well, maybe the business wasn't so good but a nice position and what a chance for something sensible and exclusive in fashion, with just the simple elegance of the name

Ruth above the shop, and nothing to follow except common sense.

I must be sensible, Ruth thought. Dear God, surely one stupid mistake was enough in her life. Now with Joseph dead and gone how could she be so unbelievably foolish as to feel like this about a man younger than herself—a man who had simply been kind enough to offer to tidy up the tiny garden for her—no, not even for her, it was part of his job anyway. At first she had been intrigued by the stories about him and Victoria Varley. To her shame she had even wondered if he had known about the theft of Joseph's money. Well, it hadn't taken her long to dismiss that idea, you looked into his face and you knew he was honest. Even the back of his head, as he listened to the sermon, was honest.

"And so, is it only this then, that St. Matthew is telling us? A simple story of faith and trust? Follow me and no questions asked? I think it is more than that," William said solemnly, turning to gaze on the cascade of the silver fishes; for a moment it broke the train of his message and he found himself wondering disconcertingly if it was going to be one of Joan's sardine Sundays. He caught her face dutifully attentive below him and hoped she might read his thoughts. It was a forlorn hope, for she had already quite decided to keep the tin of ham for a rainy day, and what on earth did William think he was talking about?

Harry Fellows didn't know either, because, in any case, he wasn't listening but looking at the American woman called April, who had picked him up in this very church and gone back to his cottage with him to get her clothes dry and talked to him about skyscrapers and tennis and hot dogs and was much more exciting in bed than Victoria Varley. And now, she sat quietly with her husband, who was rich and looking for antiques to furnish their second home which had a garage for three cars and a swimming pool. The swimming pool did not appeal to Harry but even one car would be nicer than a motorbike.

"It is the priceless gift of choice," William said. "The right to decide one's own destiny at a moment's notice. Did Simon who was called Peter or Andrew his brother say, 'Yes, well Jesus, we do see that it's important, but you know we can't just drop everything like this! Now be fair old chap, we shall have to go home first and tell our nearest and dearest in case they should worry about us and we must warn our neighbours and the trades people? No, not at all, not a bit of it. St. Matthew is quite explicit—they went straightway, they did what they wanted to do because they were free people in a free land."

Some of the congregation were already composing themselves for sleep. Most were engaged in their own private thoughts.

Webber sat with Mrs. Thomas and gave William his full attention.

Benjamin Lamb gave the new altar-piece his full attention.

Mrs. Fronefield would have liked a quick nap but found it difficult to relax when this clergyman was speaking so earnestly and so loudly. On the whole she was not impressed. The garish coloured windows and the gaudy painting, to say nothing of the clashing colours on William's surplice, were, she considered, excessive and rather Jewish.

Joan Coley recognised William in a campaigning spirit and hovered between admiration and apprehension.

William had moved around the Sea of Galilee and now glared balefully at the pews dozing on duty. "Don't think that there were no gossips in Galilee, just as there are many among us here in Flaxfield."

The pews rustled into consciousness and listened.

"When a free woman exercises her priceless gift of choice and goes about her legitimate business like Simon called

Peter and like Andrew his brother, even takes the trouble to leave a note for the milkman, then it behoves us all to remember that gossip is an evil that can wither the tender plant of truth."

William paused, partly for dramatic effect and partly to allow the heaviest sleepers to be nudged into full attention. He wondered if Harry would recognise himself as a tender plant of truth and doubted it. The lad was an innocent; there was no guile in him.

Joan Coley's apprehension had deepened into something close to panic. It was all very well for William but sometimes he forgot that she, too, lived in Flaxfield. William didn't have to do the shopping and explain his sermons as she did.

"My friends, there are people among us here in this congregation . . ." William thundered.

Joan bent her head back to a remarkable angle and gave him the concentrated glare of one of her most earnest entreaties.

William faltered and reconsidered. Perhaps she was right; she so often was. He smoothed back the wild wings of his hair and allowed the righteous blaze of indignation in his eyes to fade into mild admonition. "Who would do well to remember . . ." Joan really could be very tiresome. A full-blooded peroration would have been very satisfying and quite like the crusading days of his youth. Their eyes met in perfect understanding. The wife of a fisherman is always lonely, he read in her look. Don't you dare be too specific and anyway it's time for lunch. Get on with it!

". . . to remember that the proper bait for men is truth and not rumour and falsehood. Follow me and I . . ."

Joan's smile was genuinely grateful. She would open the tin of ham for lunch after all.

EIGHTEEN

''Her name isn't Lamb anymore than he is a doctor,'' Snow said. ''Once the FBI checked the fingerprints it was easy. April Schittski, tried for unlawful homicide or whatever they call it, certainly not for murder. She was acquitted on a plea of self-defence and took up with a shady art dealer called Lamb. They have no record for him over there. No convictions anyway.''

''But over here?'' Webber said.

''He's British; he did four years in Parkhurst for manslaughter. Billy Hummel. He was an art burglar, paintings mostly. He was surprised by a householder with a gun and in the struggle it went off the wrong way. When he came out he changed his name to Lamb—not legally, of course, that's his alias in our records. He very carelessly used it on a false passport to get to the States. Over there he seems to have gone straight, if you can call art dealing straight. Nothing they could pin on him, anyway. He'll get a shock when he tries to get back. They don't like forged passports. Any use?''

''It should be,'' Webber said unenthusiastically. ''I've got a missing woman who had a visit from a picture dealer. He had a heart attack and died on her lavatory, natural causes, no question. His wife says he should have had about twenty thousand pounds in cash on him when he died but it disappeared.''

"There's a bottle of malt on the sideboard," Betty Snow said, smiling at them possessively. "You can play shop while I wash up."

In the kitchen she reflected that if Lizzie Thomas had come with him it would have been more fun. Without her the boys were better off on their own. She still thought of them as "the boys." On the radio a plummy-voiced actor was reading Sherlock Holmes as "A Book at Bedtime." Conan Doyle would have learned a lot from a policeman's wife, she decided.

Over their whisky, Snow listened patiently while Webber filled him in.

"It doesn't fit, does it?" he said at last. "Not with the Lambs, anyway. They couldn't have killed her; the timing's wrong."

Webber nodded sadly. "Bloody tempting, though, all the stuff about the painting and both of them art dealers with a record of violence."

"And you'd have a job pinning the gallery job on them, too," Snow said. "A good counsel would tell a jury that she ate the Hershey bar when they went to see Mrs. Fronefield in the gallery. He'd say it could easily have been blown down to the basement or else it stuck to someone's shoes and got down there like that. 'Members of the jury, can you seriously believe . . . ' "

"Spare me, please," Webber sighed.

"And Mrs. Fronefield recognised them in church?"

"Yes, and Ruth the daughter did. Lamb, anyway. He'd done business with her husband before. Joseph Greenwood was really only a glorified runner. He knew that Lamb would pay well for a painting by Stanley Spencer, pay cash, a lot of cash, and no questions asked. Ruth has no illusions about her husband; he didn't like paying tax."

"And the painting is a fake," Snow said.

"A copy anyway. It looks very impressive over the altar and at a distance."

Betty came in from the washing-up and poured herself a drink.

"It was good enough to give Greenwood a heart attack," Snow said.

"Yes, but he was in a bad way already."

"Why did he want to bring Lamb into it?"

"Well, tax, for one thing, as I said, but apart from that Greenwood would have paid peanuts for it if he could. If he'd put a Spencer into public auction he'd have got world-wide publicity. He wouldn't want either the Teasdale woman or Victoria Varley screaming to the press that they'd been cheated. With Lamb he'd get what he asked and the painting would go straight to America. No publicity, not over here, anyway."

"So Lamb had no idea where Greenwood was when he died."

"Not very likely, is it? Our Joseph wouldn't want him down there. I think he'd just teased him with the name of Stanley Spencer to get his juices going."

"And Lamb found out where he was by chatting up Ruth's mother."

"That's it, and I reckon he thought he'd check out the gallery to make sure the painting wasn't there before he took off for Suffolk."

"What was Mrs. Fronefield's reaction when she saw them in church?"

"A pleasant little chat outside after the service, all very much an English country scene. Why not? They'd already told her they were going to Suffolk, apparently," Webber said gloomily, "and anyway she's still convinced that she was the victim of black Africa."

"But the real bugger is that Victoria Varley had gone missing before they got down there?"

"Yes."

"Pity to rule them out."

"I know. Nothing's neat and tidy, is it? They should have been prime suspects. The painting should have disappeared and so should they. It would all be much less confusing without them."

"As it is," Betty said, "only the actress is missing."

"She's dead," Webber said with conviction. "She's overdue with her rent on her London flat and her agent hasn't heard a word from her. She used to phone him at least once a week. He was trying to fix something for her, too. No, she's very dead somewhere, as dead as your Welsh farmer's wife, Ted, and you can't find her either."

"Her husband says she's gone off with someone. He reckons she's keeping quiet just to embarrass him. She did it once before, went off with someone, I mean, so he's got quite a good story."

"But you don't believe it," Webber said.

"Village gossip, you wouldn't credit— Sorry, of course you would. Pity the local troops didn't call us in earlier. It's probably too late now, unless he does something silly."

"Every local force likes a body; she might turn up."

"He's a pig farmer; he makes his own sausages. A nice, modern German machine. He got a government grant to buy it, too. He's quite proud of it. He told me that it uses everything except the squeal. He's got a fancy woman as well."

"No wonder they gossiped. What about forensic tests?"

"The machine is cleaned by superheated steam. You know how hygienic the Germans are. Most of his stuff is sold locally and you can't keep sausages on the shelf for long. By the time they called the Yard they'd all been eaten. Quite neat really. Something new, anyway. No sausage factories in Flaxfield?''

''No, thank God, but she's down there somewhere. Are you going back to Wales?''

''No. It'll stay on the files, of course. Perhaps his girl-friend will suddenly start wearing his wife's jewellery. Anyway, I've had enough of Wales for a bit.''

''How is Lizzie?'' Betty said hastily.

Webber grinned. ''She thinks the vicar might be in love with the church handyman, a young lad called Harry Fellows. He was Victoria Varley's boy-friend; we checked him out in C.R.O.s. Remember?''

''Just because he hasn't got a record doesn't put him in the clear. I'd have him on my list; better than your poor little Lambs, any day,'' Snow said.

''And a lot of the locals would agree with you, that's what upset the vicar. Fellows is his blue-eyed boy. Coley gave us all a good dressing down in a sermon, no less.''

''I've forgotten,'' Snow said. ''What did we do, just run a search on him as Harry Fellows?''

''Yes.''

Snow grunted. ''If its an alias he would still have showed up. Unless he's using a new name altogether, you might try getting his prints on something; no harm in another check.''

''Sure, why not, but I don't think we'll find him there. I'm not saying he's not mixed up in it somehow but I don't think he could have killed her. He's got a damn good cover, as good as you'll get anywhere.''

''Attacked from the pulpit! What fun you do have,'' Betty said, looking dubiously at the pullover she was struggling to knit before her husband's birthday. ''At least Ted only had to put up with the local paper. Had you been bullying the poor boy?''

''Not so's you'd notice, but Ted's right, he was on my list, on the top of it. Well, he would be, wouldn't he? Victoria Varley was supposed to be at a dinner party at the vicarage one night but she didn't show. Fellows turned up at the kitchen door asking if she was there. He said he hadn't seen her for a few days and said he was worried about her. In fact, she had been seen alive earlier that evening. Lizzie found a neighbour who had talked to her in Warren Lane about eight o'clock, but she's never been seen since. It was the night she was supposed to phone her agent at ten o'clock, to know whether or not she'd got a job. She never phoned and no actress would miss a phone call like that. I think she was killed some time after eight o'clock that evening but Fellows couldn't have been anywhere near her."

"Alibis aren't all that fool-proof, John; you taught me that."

"He was playing darts in a pub in Flaxfield. That's a good four miles away from Warren Lane."

"Witnesses can be unreliable. They can get dates mixed up."

"He was playing with our local village copper. They were together all the evening from about six o'clock onwards. I checked and Sergeant Burnstead is quite certain. Harry Fellows told him that he was afraid that Victoria Varley was avoiding him. Burnstead thinks he was probably right and that the lad's attention was beginning to embarrass her. He gave Harry a lift to the vicarage where Harry knew Miss Varley was asked for dinner. When she wasn't there they drove to her place, Fox House in Warren Lane. It was all properly locked up and dark. She had left a note for the milkman cancelling until further notice but that could have been an old note the killer had found lying around the house. Her car is still in the garage there but she often used the bus or a train—she didn't like driving except in the country."

"Have you officially reported her missing?" Betty asked.

"Sergeant Burnstead mentioned it in his report to the local headquarters. It's the silly season for anti-nuclear demonstrators. We've got quite a few American air-force bases in East Anglia; it uses up a lot of policemen. Besides, Victoria Varley has gone away before without telling anyone—like your farmer's wife, Ted."

"I do wish I could be clever and write a book," Betty said, "but then, nobody would believe in a sausage factory, I suppose. Coley is an unusual name, isn't it? He's my bet for you, John, the mad vicar who kills his boy-friend's lover and then steals her ill-gotten gains to buy pictures for the church."

"Coley came to Flaxfield when I was still in the force," Webber said. "He's well enough liked, a good man, as much as anyone is good, and anyway the painting was a gift; it didn't cost him a penny."

"Ted, bend your elbow and let me see if this sleeve is long enough yet," Betty said imperturbably. "Just because someone is good, kind, and loved, doesn't mean they're not mad. My mother used to give the local kids a ten-pound note to buy sweets."

"Very generous," Webber smiled. "I'll bet she was popular."

"They adored her, followed her round like a wolf pack. She'd been doing it every day for months before we found out. It's a question of degree, isn't it? Oh dear, why do I never order enough wool?"

Webber remembered Joan Coley saying cheerfully that her husband was as mad as a hatter, and Coley himself, in the pulpit, with his wild but curiously inconclusive sermon. He decided that a little malt whisky went a long way to leading you into the realms of fantasy. He pulled his mind back to facts.

"Did you tell the Kensington police about the Lambs, Ted?"

"I wasn't sure what was happening your end until we'd spoken. I didn't want to mess anything up for you."

"Why not, there's nothing to mess up, is there? You could tell them where they are, too, for all I care. If the Lambs had a visit and a few questions asked about fingerprints it would at least concentrate their minds wonderfully. They could always chat to them about passports, too."

Webber had been back in Flaxfield for six days during which time he managed to get Harry's fingerprints without arousing his suspicion. He packed the discarded cigarette packet in a plastic bag and posted it off to Snow. It was a time for waiting. He tended his garden and was content to be patient. Mrs. Thomas tended her large circle of friends and acquaintances. Like all good cooks she disliked waste and was loth to discard gossip without wondering if, like chicken stock, it might come in useful.

"Mrs. Fronefield is a nice woman," she told Webber, as they walked in the lanes around the village one evening. "She's been worried about her daughter, but that's nothing new. I'm only surprised that my Doreen hasn't made a fool of herself over Harry. Pretty boys can be murder in a village full of women."

"Is Ruth really serious about him?" Webber asked.

"She told her mother that he repelled her, but then she kept on telling her, so Thelma thinks yes, it was serious."

"Was?"

"Harry has been seeing a lot of Lamb's wife. Lamb is much easier to say than her real name, isn't it?"

"Much."

"I know they're probably not married but Lamb seems to

have encouraged it. At least Harry has been in the house with both of them. Shall we call in The Bull on our way home?''

The front parlour bar was empty apart from Betsey Trottwood with his arms round a sobbing Joan Coley.

''Whisky, I think, John, there's a dear. I haven't been able to get to the bar yet. Poor Joan is terribly upset. I'm afraid something rather nasty has happened.''

NINETEEN

''She is much better, thank heaven,'' Coley said as Joan closed the study door behind her. ''Goodness, we are honoured! That smells very much like real coffee. We usually only run to instant these days.''

''I'm glad she's better,'' Webber said. ''Mr. Trottwood was quite worried about her; we all were. It must have been very unpleasant for her.''

It was over a week since Joan had succumbed to mild hysterics in the parlour bar of The Bull. Mrs. Thomas had not been idle and from her Webber had probably a fair picture of what had happened and between them they had sorted out what seemed to be the facts from the more lurid flights of village fancy. The painting had been stolen from the church and there was no doubt that it had been stolen by Dr. Lamb and his wife. It had been found abandoned in their house. A close inspection had obviously shown it to be nothing but a poor copy. They had taken their car and cleared off as quickly as they could. His visit to Coley Webber had deliberately left until now. He had no wish to be identified with the official enquiries that Sergeant Burnstead had initiated.

"She was lucky," Webber said. "She could have easily disturbed them and that could have been dangerous. They both have records of violence, I believe."

"Poor creatures," Coley said. "Yes, so the police told Sergeant Burnstead. Well, mercifully there was no question of that. It seems to have been a straight-forward robbery. I see the *Anglian Recorder* rather melodramatically refers to it as sacrilege."

"But accurately, surely?"

"If one wants to appeal to sensationalism—yes, I suppose so." Coley sipped his coffee and Webber saw that his hand was shaking. It showed the strain he had undergone. "I deplore the press, John, I'm afraid. It has a false morality. The man who wrote that wasn't thinking of the violation of a holy church, he was looking for a headline and a pat on the back from his editor. It wouldn't occur to him to wonder and to pity the poor devils who could shame themselves so terribly."

"Does that mean," Webber said, "that you won't press charges when they pick them up?"

"Mercifully I won't have to. I understand the police will do that anyway. To be honest, I'm rather hoping they will have left the country by now. They can be extradited, I'm told, but since we have recovered the painting I rather got the impression that the matter will be allowed to drop. Their car was found outside the local office of the car-hire firm in Norwich, I believe. That, at least, shows some basic decency, wouldn't you think?"

Norwich was also on the main rail link to London, Webber thought, and the car-hire people were almost opposite the railway station. "Yes, I suppose so," he said. "Did the officers say when you would get the painting back?"

"Sergeant Burnstead collected it from them this morning. I have asked him to take it to Mr. Trottwood, who is already very kindly repairing the frame. Ah, Joan dear! Yes, quite finished, thank you. Delicious. The frame was in a terrible state but luckily the painting itself seems to be unharmed."

"I had just been checking the flower rota in the porch," Joan said, collecting the cups. "At first I thought someone had been deliberately attacking the altar—there were bits of the frame all over it—but William thinks they let the painting fall when they were getting it down. I wish I could get my hands on them!"

"My dear!" Coley reproved her mildly. "We really mustn't confuse clumsiness with desecration."

"Poor Joan," Mrs. Thomas said, when Webber told her. "Coley is either potty or a saint and I wouldn't much care to live with either."

"Are you sure the pool will be open at this time of the year?" Webber asked resignedly, as they drove to Dunwold.

"You only read the paper for news. You should look at the adverts: 'Why go to Spain? Dunwold's Holiday Camp is now open from March onwards. Swim in our heated tropical lagoon and relax in the luxury of our Hawaiian restaurant.' By rights, you should be swimming in Italy. This ought to be just as good for your arthritis and no mosquitoes. You'll enjoy it when you get there, you'll see. We could do with an evening out, it's ages since we went to Dunwold."

"Last summer, and it was too cold to swim. It nearly always is, thank God."

"We're not going in the sea. A nice, warm indoor pool surrounded by exotic tropical trees. They're only plastic, I'm told but, fair play, you can't expect real ones, can you?"

"You seem remarkably well informed."

"I know one of the girls who works in the restaurant. She used to be in the Co-op in Flaxfield. She does part time at the moment. They're training her for full time in the summer. Sharon Ball. She used to be one of Burnstead's old flames until he settled down. Nice enough but a bit dim."

The road wound down to the coast, narrow and quiet in the fading light.

"Joan said that Coley was very impressed that the police got on to the Lambs so quickly."

"Coley impresses easily," Webber said. "They didn't come because of the robbery, they came on a tip-off from Ted Snow, and it took them long enough. Did you manage to discover why Gough was there at the house when they arrived? He was very cagey when Burnstead asked him."

"Mr. Gough is the great 'I am.' " Mrs. Thomas chuckled. "He considers himself a cut above village policemen. He was probably a bit embarrassed, too. He had a sale the day before. He was selling Mrs. Teasdale's stuff. I think he was hoping to push the price up on her father's paintings but Lamb never turned up and they didn't interest the ring so Betsey bought them. Gough would know better than to try anything on him; Betsey knows all Gough's tricks. Anyway, Gough was curious to know why Lamb never showed up. He was on the doorstep when the detectives arrived."

"Surely no cause to embarrass such a solid citizen?"

"The Lamb woman had been complaining about the earth lavatory at the bottom of the garden ever since they moved in."

"A bit too pongy for her?"

"The whole idea of it came as a shock. Apparently they don't have them in America. I haven't found out how much rent Gough was charging them. Plenty, knowing that crafty devil. It was all in cash, anyway. I know the girl in Gough's office, but she doesn't know how much, either. Rich Americans were a good contact for him. He would want to keep in with them.''

''Lizzie, stop waffling.''

''Gough had promised to supply them with a new chemical lavatory. The police arrived and found him with it on the doorstep. I think he felt it was a bit beneath his dignity.''

Webber grinned at the image of the self-important Gough in the role of sanitary engineer and errand boy. ''And the Lambs had skipped off with a flick of their tails. How do you like it for size?'' he asked.

Mrs. Thomas clutched her handbag on her lap and saw the hedgerows leap into clear light as Webber switched on the headlamps.

''It makes sense at first, but only a bit of it, not everything.''

''Go on,'' he said.

''Lamb wanted the painting. He could cope with a dealer or even a private owner but a painting over an altar is different. There's not much he could do except steal it and he was well qualified to do just that.''

Webber nodded. ''Because, like Greenwood and like Betsey, he thought it might be the real thing. Then he has a good close look when he gets it home. All right so far?''

''It wouldn't take him long to see it was wrong, so they take off in a hurry. It's the end of a wild goose chase, so the sooner they clear off the better. After all, Lamb was on pretty shaky ground over here. He'd left a broken frame all over the altar. He'd know the police would be called in and start asking questions. Ruth and her mother staying in the village would make him feel uneasy, too. Yes, it makes sense up to there.''

The road lifted on to a gentle rise and in the distance they could see the lights of Dunwold, stopped short by the black arc of the invisible sea.

"So why don't you like it, Lizzie?"

"All right, so the painting is a rubbishy old copy, but why leave it behind to connect them with the church? Why not dump it or burn it, or even take it with them? Anything but leave it. People might have thought they'd left rather suspiciously, I suppose, but you couldn't prove anything. That's what I don't like."

Webber nodded unhappily but said nothing until the car threaded its way through the quiet streets of the town and out on to the exit road which led to the north cliffs, where a group of buildings and chalets crouched bravely in the wind. The biggest block had once been a Victorian hotel. Now as the brochures proudly stated, "Completely refurbished," it had been gutted to accommodate the unlikely combination of the Tropical Lagoon and Leisure Centre.

Webber disliked swimming intensely and cursed the day when Sarah Collins had told Mrs. Thomas that it was good for him. He changed and sat miserably at the edge of the water, waiting for her. The Tropical Lagoon, for all its brave attempt to defy the English climate and simulate Hawaii, remained exactly what it was: an oval swimming pool with steaming water of an impossible blue surrounded by plastic palms of an impossible green. The summer visitors had not yet arrived and there were only a few brave young locals self-consciously ploughing through the mists. From time to time someone opened a door and swept the mist away with a blast of icy wind from the North Sea. He decided that it was warmer in than out, and it was. He saw her from the pool before she saw him and not for the first time was inexplicably filled with an emotion very close to love, although it wasn't perhaps the word he himself would have chosen. Bravery was a quality he much admired and, as he watched her now, a short plump figure in her one-piece swim suit with zig-zag stripes of green and blue, defiant above the prominent veins of her stubby legs, supremely contemptuous of the wounding grins of the local youth around her, he felt like crying "bravo!" She dived in with unexpected grace and surfaced near him like a submarine wearing wartime camouflage. It seemed right and fitting to kiss her. It was a clumsy kiss and landed mostly on her nose. She acknowledge it with a shy grin and a wink of deep delight as they set off for their exercise to a background of taped guitars.

On the floor above the pool the tables of the Honolulu restaurant, sheltered behind glass, looked down on the palm trees and the swimmers through the steam. Floating exhausted on his back in the deep end, Webber thought he saw two faces he knew as the steam momentarily cleared but when he next had a chance to see clearly the table was empty.

"Perhaps I was wrong," he said, as they looked at the menu in the bar later. "I only saw them for a moment. How does chopped suckling pig and pineapple in dainty parcels of vine leaves strike you?"

"Not a lot. Sharon reckons that the grilled ham is the best bet, and I don't think you were wrong. Sharon says they've been out here for dinner two or three times lately."

Webber glanced through the wine list wondering what would best survive the spices of the Pacific. It was good of Lizzie to suggest an evening out, although the food could hardly be to her liking, any more than a foggy swim had been to his. It was interesting seeing Harry Fellows dining intimately with Ruth Greenwood, although the fact that they had done so was surely something Lizzie could have told him without dragging him here to witness it for himself. There was something else. He went back over the conversation of the evening, eliminating and checking.

"Sharon Ball," he said conversationally. " 'Nice enough, but a bit dim,' you said. Been seeing a lot of her, have you?"

She eyed him with respect. "Quite a bit. She lives here during the week but comes back to Flaxfield at weekends until she's trained and working full time. I'd like to know what you think of her."

"Because you think she might not be all that dim?"

"I told you she was one of Sergeant Burnstead's old flames. He's dropped her now and she doesn't like it. You're better with women than I am."

"Lizzie, you can hardly expect me to quiz the poor girl over jumbo prawns and okra soup."

"You know I don't expect that. Jealousy can make people talk. Just tell me what you think of her."

"It looks as if we'll have to wait a while to get served," Webber said. "You'd best tell me just what it is that you are going to ask me to believe."

He listened to her attentively and when, at last, after a long wait, Sharon Ball arrived to take their order, Webber looked at her with considerable interest. She was dressed in an ill-fitting uniform of white nylon with the skirt overprinted to suggest plaited grass. With Mrs. Thomas she was easy and chatted freely about the menu. She was less sure of herself with Webber and the wine list.

He smiled at her encouragingly. "Have you got a white Macon?" he enquired kindly.

She scowled down at her uniform. "It's a sort of nylon overall," she said resignedly.

At least, he thought, she didn't suffer from an overactive imagination. He didn't believe that what she had told Lizzie was prompted by jealousy either. She was, he considered, a girl who accepted defeat with resignation.

Dunwold didn't boast anything so dramatic as cliffs; only a

modest embankment with a coast path kept the winter storms away from the straggle of buildings along the front. There were a few shelters where the summer visitors could sit on hard wooden benches and look at the sea. Now they were empty except for the one where Harry sat with Ruth after their Hawaiian dinner.

I haven't done this, she thought, since I was sixteen and went to Jersey with Mummy and Daddy and they came looking for me and made me go back to the hotel. She remembered the shame she'd felt, not for herself, but for her mother and father. The boy had never written to her. He promised he would, but he hadn't. Now she remembered the same hard wooden seat and the sound of the sea filling the darkness of the shelter and she felt the same tightness in her stomach. It had never felt like that again, not until now. Certainly never with poor Joe, who had only been the key to escape from her parents.

When Harry cupped his hands to light a cigarette he reminded her of a portrait by Joseph Wright. It was hardly the sort of compliment that would mean anything to him. Perhaps she should tell him that he made her stomach feel tight.

Instead she said, "You don't mind when we go out, that I pay for everything? I don't embarrass you?"

"No"—he sounded surprised but not embarrassed—"why should I? I like being with you and I haven't got enough money to pay for us. I don't mind if you don't."

A bit puzzled, that was the best tack, but open and honest. Ruth liked it when he was truthful and spoke out; she'd told him that and she was right—he liked her for it. He liked her for all sorts of things; she could laugh and she was easy to be with. Useful, too.

"Did you sleep with Victoria? Victoria Varley?"

"She wanted me to." He grinned sheepishly. "The thing is— Well, yes, we tried it but I couldn't get— It was no good,

I couldn't. So I reckon that's what we did all right—we just slept."

Ruth was very pretty when she laughed like that. He laughed with her to show that he didn't mind even though it was a bit private and personal. She'd know it hadn't been his fault, though; she'd know that. That's why she was laughing and he could laugh with her because he was open and honest.

And Ruth could be kind, too, like the time he'd told her all about his early life in the orphanage. In his mind the orphanage had become very real to him. She'd been sorry for him then, and even a bit near to tears when he'd remembered losing his mam and dad when he was only a toddler. Well, she would understand, losing her own husband like that. They couldn't have been real close though, not knowing about all that money he'd been carrying. Perhaps she had so much money in the bank that she hadn't even missed it. A shop in London could make you rich. It could if you knew about paintings, it could. If you knew the good ones from the bad copies. Not like the Yanks—they couldn't tell shit from sugar, not until they'd seen it right up close, they couldn't, and then they'd only given him fifty rotten quid for nicking it from the church for them, mean bastards. Only that wasn't for laughing about with Ruth, not like poking gentle fun at poor old Vicky.

"Truth is," he said, "I reckon that's why she's flit off for a bit. She wouldn't talk about it, not open and straight out, she wouldn't. Funny, that. You wouldn't think she'd be shy, being on the telly an' all, would you? But she is. It never worried me. She was the one; she worried. Daft old thing, all that money and worrying."

"Does she have money?" She kept the sharpness she felt out of her voice so that there was only polite interest in it.

"She's a close one. Not that I cared. Her business, not mine. Live and let live I say. One week she'd moan about no money to pay her tax and the next she'd start talking about—what was it? Investing? Aye, that's right, investing in some theatre play or something. Someone in Ireland she had to see and then perhaps someone in America. Cost a lot in travel, that would. Yes, she's got money all right. I reckon she's stinking." Did that sound too crude? Or even disloyal? "She's a nice woman, though," he said sincerely. "I like her."

Ruth didn't care any more what he thought about Victoria Varley. She didn't care about the rest of his life either or the questions teased out of jealousy that she had sometimes wanted to ask him about the Lamb woman and time he'd spent with her. Who could blame anyone for being attracted to him? She couldn't remember moving closer to him but she was so happy that she didn't care and it was wonderful to sit and feel him close with the warmth of his body near her, with no need to say anything, while far out on the black sea they could watch the lights of the Dunwold fishing boats.

It was good for Harry, too. Good to feel trusted and needed. Only he wasn't going to be so crude as to try anything, not here. One day it would be nice for her to need him and trust him when they were alone in London. When her mother had gone home, because her mother didn't like him, and that was a pity, but nothing he couldn't get round. London was the place. In London people wouldn't poke and pry or want to know about your money. He pictured himself helping Ruth in her own shop, her own gallery. No one questioned people who worked in a picture gallery, like her husband who had died with his pockets stuffed full of it, like the Yank with his briefcase so full he could hardly close it. No, not here. No sense in being crude and spoiling everything, and old man Coley would see that this way was best for him, too, and let him go. "I only want the best for you," that's what he'd said. "Only the best for you, old fellow. Hullo, old fellow. Keeping your pecker up?'' Always ''old fellow,'' and then later laughing and planning a quiet life for him. ''Fellows, that's it! We'll call you Fellows,'' He'd want the best for him; he'd still want that for him. He had pins and needles in his leg.

''Won't your mam be worrying about you being so late?''

For an instant she pictured her mother outside looking for her and shining a torch into every dark corner. There was no torch, and no one had come near them. Her mother could never do that to her again.

Harry stood to ease the pain in his leg and she stood with him and held him close to her. He tried to remember some of the things the woman had written in her novel. There were things you were supposed to say to girls like Ruth, nice girls, but everything he remembered sounded silly.

He kissed her gently and settled for, ''It's late. I'll take you home.''

She had no intention of going home, not yet, not when she was so obviously doing better than Victoria Varley had done.

TWENTY

Eight days later it was Webber's birthday. He knew perfectly well that Mrs. Thomas hadn't forgotten but he gave her the pleasure of surprising him.

''The first course, we're having here,'' she announced, as they sat in The Bull sharing a bottle of champagne. ''I asked them to order some smoked salmon from Orford. Just a few sandwiches to get the juices going, not too filling. The rest is doing nicely in the oven for us at home. I can't bear that great con trick in restaurants, one damn great plate of food after another. I'm like you, I like to spread it out."

"I hope," Webber smiled seriously, "that you are referring to food and not to my waistline or the mystery of the missing actress."

"I wouldn't talk shop on your birthday. Cheers."

"Cheers. I know you have a thicker skin than I have, but doesn't it worry you guzzling smoked salmon and champagne in here?"

"Certainly not. It's very good for the locals to see how the rich live. Knowing you, however, I have arranged for any of your friends who might drop in to be asked discreetly to order anything they like to drink to your health. That way they can raise their glasses respectfully at a distance without feeling that they have to join us. Part of your birthday treat, let's say."

She should have been a lady of the manor, he thought, and in a way perhaps she was. Not that she considered herself superior and she certainly wasn't snobbish. If such a word existed then she was probably a meritocrat—brighter than most and knew it, but not, thank God, so that it showed.

"You can hardly call our modest resources a fortune," he said, "unless you've been lucky with one of your five Premium Bonds."

"People have been known to win with just one, but that's not my kind of luck. Do you remember Andy Baldwin?"

Webber dredged back in his memory, interrupted in his efforts by several cheerful toasts to his health from acquaintances at the bar across the room. "The kid policeman at Kensington, when they did the Greenwood Gallery?"

"That's the one. I've kept in touch. He's a bright boy; I liked him."

"So did I," Webber said solemnly, "but I hadn't thought of writing. Why does champagne give you such a quick lift, I wonder. Are you perhaps going to tell me that your bright boy has been working nights and come up with some of the answers to our problem?"

"You don't get much chance to play detectives if you're a copper on the beat, remember? He isn't settling down very well. Doesn't like life in the section house; doesn't like the police very much, either. It wasn't so bad when he could get home once in a while to see his mam and dad. He was the only son. He'll miss them. They were both killed in a car smash on the motorway about ten days ago."

"Poor man," Webber said, unconsciously promoting Andy Baldwin to the sorrows of adult life. "All the same, the section-house life won't last for ever. With unemployment like it is he could do worse."

"He's been on sick leave for the funeral and settling things up and he's already given in his notice."

"Did they leave him a fortune, then?"

"No; a few thousand in the Post Office. Not enough to live on, let alone retire. He had four hundred pounds of his own and one Premium Bond."

Webber put back the last of his smoked salmon sandwich on his plate, unfinished. "You're going to tell me that just one Premium Bond was enough?"

"Would you have chucked the force if your number had come up in the draw?"

"How much did he win?"

"I didn't like to ask, but enough to make him think hard about what he wants to do with his life, apparently. He's probably collected the big one—how much is it now? One hundred thousand pounds? So what would you have done?"

"You can certainly mess up a plate of birthday sandwiches, Lizzie. How do I know, for God's sake. I never had the chance to decide, did I?"

"You might have the chance to do it by proxy. I've told him he's welcome to come and stay with me for a bit until he can get himself straight. At least some decent food won't hurt him."

She had always liked stray dogs. Perhaps with Doreen not being the son she had wanted it was an unconscious and frustrated maternal instinct, Webber thought.

"It's to be the other part of my birthday treat," he said resignedly. "You've got him in the kitchen wearing a pinny and basting the joint."

"Don't be daft," she beamed, delighted that he wanted to eat alone with her. "He probably won't want to come anyway and it isn't a joint, it's a pot roast. Does Harry Fellows rate a free drink, d'you think? I see the barman raising his eyebrows at you."

Webber hadn't noticed Harry come in. He nodded to the barman. Unversed in local etiquette, Harry walked over and raised his pint of beer. "Happy birthday, Mr. Webber."

"Thank you, Harry. Keeping busy, then?"

"There's always something—and a bit on the side, if I'm lucky."

"Perks?"

"A bit of gardening over and above, like. Odd jobs. Hedges are sprouting up nicely now the weather's warmer. There's not a fortune in odd jobs, Mr. Webber, even if you get paid."

"Don't tell me you get bad debts in Flaxfield?"

"Sometimes. Did a bit for those Yanks, didn't I?"

"The Lambs?"

"Sergeant reckons that weren't their name, not proper.

Seems they thought the vicar's painting was worth a fortune."

"Sergeant Burnstead told you?"

"All over Flaxfield, that is. Owed the shops as well as me. Crafty. No wonder they flit. I cleared a pile of rotten old apples out the cupboards and wardrobe for them, got a cup of coffee and a promise of ten pounds. Not much of a perk, you might say. Cheers! Be coming up to planting time soon, Mr. Webber. You let me know if you need a hand."

"Thank you, Harry, I will."

As if aware for the first time that Mrs. Thomas had been staring at him silently, Harry Fellows turned his handsome face to her and smiled. It was a good smile, she thought; spontaneous, with a hint of shyness that made him lower his thick eyelashes before nodding to them politely and retiring to the crowd round the bar.

"It's not everyone gets wished a happy birthday by a murderer," she said, pouring the last of the wine evenly between their glasses. "Fair play, though, he's a good looker but then I've never trusted Alsatian dogs either. Hungry?"

"Yes, come on. What about the vegetables?"

"All done. Your favourite, a purée of swedes and potatoes in butter with a pinch of nutmeg, five minutes in the oven while I lay the table."

Webber was quiet during the meal but he left nothing on his plate and she let him take his time until he lit his pipe and they finished the washing-up.

"They don't always make mistakes, do they?" she said. "I mean you must have known people who killed and got away with it."

"Far more than you hear about, which is why you don't hear about them."

"Ones who weren't even suspected?"

"Oh, God knows how many of those, but more than enough of the ones we did suspect."

"It's a fair old time now since Victoria Varley disappeared and there's no official murder, no police investigation. If Harry Fellows killed her and took the money, why doesn't he just pack his bags and disappear himself somewhere?"

"There's no murder chase, Lizzie, because officially there is no murder. The thing is, love, that no one cares and, poor woman, I don't suppose anyone ever really did care much about her either. Not that crook of an agent, anyway. And in the end the flat owners in Chelsea will just be glad to get rid of a sitting tenant. They'll tart the place up and let it for a lot more money. Thousands of women disappear regularly every year, it's difficult to believe but it's true. Sometimes a body floats up from the bottom of a lake or someone opens a cupboard door and finds a mummified body."

"Joan Coley thinks Harry looks like the Michelangelo Adam. There's a print in Coley's study," she said.

"She thinks or Coley thinks?" Webber said teasingly. "No, Lizzie, I reckon that's not one of your best ideas. Coley may well be a bit cranky but he's not kinky. Perhaps Harry will turn out to be his illegitimate son from his wild-oat days at Oxford."

"That would hardly account for Joan's feeling for him, though, would it? Although I don't know, she's daft enough, I suppose. Dear me, why don't you have nice black and white characters in your cases?" she sighed.

"What's wrong with Harry? Just because he's a good-looking bastard doesn't stop him being a villain. Can you rely on the girl—what's her name? Sharon, Sharon Ball—not to say anything?"

"Yes, I think so. I suppose you'll have to speak to Sergeant Burnstead sooner or later?"

"It would be nice not to, wouldn't it? Perhaps Harry will be a good boy and make a mistake, so that I won't have to."

"Like killing Ruth Greenwood?"

"I reckon him bad but he's not mad. Besides she hasn't got any money. I don't see him as a sex maniac. I think he goes for money."

"What about her mother? She's not poor and she'd probably leave it to Ruth."

"You are a cheerful soul, aren't you? No, he's too clever. He might marry her, of course, and see Mummy off later. I can't see him in an art gallery, though, can you?"

"With those looks and a good suit—yes, I can. He'd soon pick up the jargon. You said he was clever."

"Yes, I think he's clever enough to be worrying. It's always worrying when people don't fit into a pattern. The rain seems to have held off. Let's get some fresh air or I shall drop off after that nice food."

Nice food was all she wanted to hear. She wouldn't have expected fulsome thanks anyway, and she was pleased because it meant that his mind was occupied with serious things.

The sky over the common was like a blanket of grey flannel but it didn't depress them.

"What kind of a pattern?" she asked, regretting that she hadn't put stouter shoes on.

"I reckon it for a nice straightforward domestic murder," Webber said. "They were close enough, that's for sure. Betsey says that Victoria was in love with him and I can believe it."

"He also says that Harry was fond of her, too. That Harry was proud to be seen with her."

"She wasn't killed for a sex murder. Anyway, it would probably have been the other way round. Older jealous women kill lovers who play around. Young men find sex for free. They can't find money so easily and twenty thousand pounds in notes is a lot of money to come knocking on the door on a snowy night."

"And you still don't think you should say anything to Ruth or her mother?"

They had come to the edge of the common, where the thick clumps of gorse gave way to the disciplined fairways and the smooth greens of the golf course. On the horizon they could see the rain falling like a curtain of gauze and moving towards them.

He didn't answer for some moments, until, choosing his words with care, he said, "No, I don't. Ruth's fascinated by his relationship with Victoria Varley. She's probably fascinated by him, too, but I think it's best to leave it."

"Like a goat tied up for a tiger."

"Oh, come on! You know that's not true. I don't see Ruth or her mother in any danger. Ruth doesn't know anything, and Harry knows she doesn't. All he's got to do is keep his mouth shut."

"And we don't know anything, either."

"Nothing we can prove," he admitted.

"Perhaps we've got it wrong."

"Sure. Why not? It wouldn't be the first time. I just don't think so, that's all, but for God's sake don't talk about goats and tigers. Harry's not a wild animal on the prowl and Ruth is the wrong kind of bait. Short term, anyway. I reckon him strictly a cash-and-carry merchant. I think that either he was there when Ruth's husband had his heart attack with a stack of notes on him or, if he wasn't, then Victoria told him about it. I think that when she talked about investing it in a play he didn't think she was very sensible and I think he killed her."

"Unless she turns up."

"She won't."

"And no other suspects."

"No; no tight little circle of anxious faces in the library

for the last scene, Lizzie. Not a nice, tidy whodunnit and not a crafty, unpredictable sex maniac.''

''Just a nice, tidy boy with long eyelashes.''

A child in the distance ignored the advancing rain and flew a kite with absorbed concentration, making it dive and soar with delight.

''No, not a who, a why or even how. I'll settle for a whereisit.''

''What we need,'' she said, looking down sadly at her soaking shoes, ''is a nice sausage factory.''

TWENTY-ONE

Dr. Collins opened the door of her surgery and bellowed into the waiting room, ''Next please! Oh, it's you Elizabeth. Thank God you're the last. Come through.''

''I made sure I was the last,'' Mrs. Thomas said comfortably, sailing into the untidy surgery and seating herself with a familiarity that indicated to Sarah at once that the visit was non-professional—although with Lizzie Thomas she had long since given up trying to separate the Hippocratic oath from friendship. As an overworked general practitioner she had had little time to cultivate personal friendship. It had taken Mrs. Thomas to realise that under the skin of the efficient medical exterior there lurked a lonely soul and a fellow gossip with a fund of useful information not generally available to the suffering public of Flaxfield.

Sarah eased her shoes off with alternate toes and washed her face gratefully at the corner wash basin, not for hygiene but as a hostess prepares to receive an old friend.

"Tea?"

"Better not; your cups always taste of carbolic." Mrs. Thomas produced two glasses, a bottle of tonic water and a quarter bottle of gin.

"Oh, Elizabeth, you are a lovely, wicked woman, thank God. What do you want?"

"It's gone six. I could have caught you in The Bull later, I suppose, but I thought this was cosier. My personal prescription. You look washed out."

"Quite right on both counts. Just a large one, then. You haven't run out of elastic stockings, I take it, and since I look like this at the end of every day—thank you, cheers. I imagine you are after something?"

"Was Mrs. Teasdale, over at Wangford, one of yours?"

"A patient? No, at least not until they got her into the Cottage Hospital. I saw her there once or twice, towards the end, when the registrar asked my advice. I don't think she had a doctor of her own. She told me she didn't like doctors much."

"What did she die of?"

"Nothing suspicious, you evil old woman. You could say that she died because her time had come."

"Who said I was suspicious?" Mrs. Thomas said virtuously. "I happened to overhear someone talking in the butchers. I didn't even know she was ill."

"She caught a cold and it got complicated with 'flu and asthma. She was badly undernourished, too. God knows what some women feed themselves on. Did you know her?"

"I met her once. A mean woman. She was undernourished because she wouldn't spend money on proper food. I just wondered why they've taken her over to Rutley, unless, of course, there's going to be a post-mortem?''

''Well, she's not full of some obscure poison, I promise you. At least, I sincerely hope not, since I signed the death certificate. Anyway, there's no question of a post-mortem. I imagine she's over in Rutley because we don't run to an undertakers in Flaxfield. It's the usual practice—they'll keep her in the freeze box until the funeral. Simple as that; nothing sinister. The undertakers collect from the hospital. You could hardly expect them to leave the poor thing coffined up in her empty cottage. Different if she'd had a family. Seems a pity to waste the rest of that tonic, Elizabeth. Drink up and I'll treat you in The Bull next time.''

It wasn't only the gin, Mrs. Thomas thought, as she sat and watched Sarah Collins unwind. She liked her lack of pretension and genuine spirit of kindness. She listened while Sarah tilted against the bureaucracy of hospital administration, the shortcomings of the National Health Service in general, and the medical profession in particular. ''Although patients run us a good second,'' Sarah concluded with gloomy satisfaction. ''They either complain too much or not enough.''

''Like Mrs. Teasdale?''

''Yes, certainly. Some decent food and an inhaler and she'd probably still be pouring tea in front of her own fire. But that's silly, of course. It goes deeper than that. You can't change people's nature—so she died.''

''Because her time had come?''

''That's it. Although I suppose we are poaching on Coley's ground now. A man well-named, Elizabeth—an odd fish if ever I saw one.''

''Kind, though?''

''Well-meaning, perhaps. He certainly does his share of

hospital visiting, even the people who don't want to be visited."

"You don't like him?"

"To be honest, I haven't really given him much thought. I suppose he does his job according to his own lights." Sarah burped gently and with satisfaction. "I find him a bit creepy. Perhaps I'm being unfair. He just seems to enjoy it all so much. He's got what I call a bedpan syndrome—all that gush about 'I was sick and ye visited me,' and so on. Sorry, forget it. I tend to get ungracious at the end of the day. I like Joan, although it must be a strain for her living with Coley; not much of a giggle. She'd live on tranquillisers if I didn't watch her. With her temperament she should have married someone quite unfanatical, someone nice and steady like your John— How is his arthritis? He should have gone to Italy, you know."

Really, there were times, Mrs. Thomas thought, when Sarah could behave more like a schoolgirl than a woman of science. "I can't see John looking twice at Joan. She'd drive him mad in a morning. Besides, she is devoted to Coley. He may be a bit potty but she must have known that when she married him. Underneath all that flutter she is basically the maternal type. John isn't too bad, you know, once I get him moving. I think he finds difficulty tying his shoe laces but he won't admit it."

So the visit was about John Webber, Sarah thought, nothing to do with the poor Teasdale woman or the vicar and his wife. It was just Elizabeth's way of putting her own mind at rest. Thank goodness she was used to the circumlocutions of her patients.

"Nothing to worry about; he'll be good for years yet. Get him shoes without laces and a long shoehorn. If he ever got really bad I could fix him up with a couple of new hips in two shakes of a lamb's tail— Is there any news of those two thieving bastards, by the way?''

''The Americans? John thinks they're probably out of the country by now. Lamb wasn't their real name, you know. He thinks they could have passports in other names, too. No, I'm not really bothered about John. Sometimes I worry that we don't have one really good pair of legs between us but I dare say we'll manage.''

She knew that Sarah thought John was the reason she had descended upon her with gin and decided that she could best confirm it by denying it.

''Anyway, your advice about the swimming was a success, I think.'' She gossiped about their visit to the pool at Dunwold and, like a fisherman trying his luck with a selection of flies, she floated the names of Sharon Ball and Sergeant Burnstead. Then, later, when they were laughing at the horrors of pseudo Hawaiian food, she tried Ruth Greenwood and Harry Fellows.

''It just makes things rather boring, that's all,'' Mr. Gough said, when Webber and Mrs. Thomas went to see him in his office the next morning. ''Not that the few things she put into the auction fetched anything, and the sale of both her father's cottage and her own won't amount to much. Since she died without leaving a will, and there are no relations of any sort, then presumably everything will eventually go to the Government.''

''If she left no will,'' Webber said, ''then how do we know she wanted to be buried with her father?''

''You are obviously like me and don't bother with such morbid customs,'' Gough said. ''Apparently it's a question of space—you can reserve it rather like a theatre ticket. That's all the hold-up is, I understand. Mrs. Teasdale didn't have a solicitor, otherwise I'm sure he would have advised her to make a will and saved us all a good deal of unnecessary paperwork.'' Gough eyed them both shrewdly.

When an ex-Inspector of Police showed an interest in someone's death there could be a reason for it. His brain was not very quick but he let it rove briefly over Mrs. Teasdale's past history; the death of her father and the sale of his goods and chattels, some of which had only recently been in his own sale-room. He thought of Victoria Varley's disappearance and the hasty departure of his American clients who had turned out to be so very disappointing. He remembered his thrill of excitement—he didn't use the word greed in his thoughts—when he had spent happy hours of anticipation driving them all over Suffolk in search of fine English paintings. Then the sad anti-climax when they had turned out to be common art thieves, and not very good ones, either, to have wasted their time and energy stealing a fake from the church. And it was very irritating to have spent so much money on the quite unnecessary purchase of that chemical lavatory.

''Have you by any chance heard whether they have stopped those American people getting out of the country?'' Gough asked, as he showed them out.

''Still owe you a bit, do they?'' Webber said.

''There are always things left outstanding, I'm afraid,'' Gough said sadly.

''So Harry Fellows was telling me. They weren't very good at paying their debts, were they? Harry try and touch you for what they owed him, did he?''

''Whatever arrangement he made with them was entirely his own affair,'' Gough said primly. ''I certainly do not intend to pay him. I don't really believe he thought I would. That young man has his eye to the main chance and he can whistle for his twenty pounds.''

Webber nodded amiably. "Quite right. I hope you managed to get the rent out of them before they left?"

"It was paid in advance," Gough said.

"Very sensible."

"Twenty pounds for a few odd jobs," Mrs. Thomas mused. "Everything is so expensive, isn't it?"

"Just you let me know if you'd like me to get the place cleaned up for you," she said, squeezing Mr. Gough's arm with gentle concern. "I quite enjoy housework and some of those local women can charge a fortune."

That evening Webber would have liked to get to bed early to ease the ache in his hips—aching mainly, he realised, because he disliked limping and felt that while he was with Lizzie it would amount to an admission of infirmity. Instead, when he had walked her home after they left The Bull, he didn't go back to the comfort of his own bed but met Sergeant Burnstead by an appointment they had made earlier. Webber took him home and talked to him over a glass of whisky. They had both made the police their chosen career, both of them were local men, and both were fundamentally decent, except that Burnstead was a decent fool and Webber was clever enough not to let it become an issue in their seemingly casual talk. With Webber, a confession could slip easily into the general conversation, and so it did, almost before the sergeant had realised it.

"Perhaps it won't have to come out," Webber said quietly, when a long silence had fallen between them, "but I had to check it, you see that?"

"Yes, I see that," the Sergeant said.

TWENTY-TWO

It wasn't morbid curiosity that promoted Mrs. Thomas' interest in funerals, it was quite simply that she enjoyed them. During the years she had lived in England she had in many ways adapted herself to the customs of her neighbours and yet she found their lack of enthusiasm for the ceremonial of death to be curiously shaming; like discovering a friend to have an inexplicable blind spot. That Mrs. Teasdale had been an unprepossessing woman, without a living relative to mourn her passing, only seemed to make it even more necessary that she should get a decent salute when she joined her father in the north churchyard of St. Peter's. It wouldn't have worried the vicar had no one turned up at all. Coley would have conducted the service as he had often done for the elderly and unloved of his flock, with the help of a churchwarden or two and perhaps one of the flower ladies who might be persuaded to attend if she happened to be working in the church at the time. In spite of the rain he was rather pleased with today's turnout. After all, the woman was in a way responsible for her father's painting finding its way to the church. It was fitting that she should join her father with a modicum of gratitude.

Some distance away, behind the low boundary wall of the churchyard, Andy Baldwin sheltered under the dripping leaves of an inadequate tree and watched the graveside ceremony with mixed feelings. Not long ago he had been part of a similar ritual and had watched the coffins of his mother and father lowered into the ground. He was surprised to find that he could watch the same service, and so soon afterwards, without feeling the sick ache of disbelief. In many ways, he was a sensitive young man and not lacking in imagination, but his strength of character—although as yet he was largely unaware of it himself—lay in his determination to follow his own star and his only emotion now, as he watched the people gathered around the empty grave, was one of pleasurable excitement that he had come to a decision.

He had felt it driving down from London through the rain, with the words of advice in Mrs. Thomas' letters filling his head. Her letters never sounded like advice; she talked to him and answered his questions, and most of his questions had been about John Webber. Webber, himself, had been unaware of the impression he had made on the young policeman. Hero worship is more usually reserved by people of Andy Baldwin's generation for pop stars and footballers and they are well served by television and the newspapers. Mrs. Thomas ran her own personal fan club unaided and when she found someone who shared her enthusiasm she could be a more powerful advocate than even she realised. The boy's determination had an element of stubbornness, even of secrecy, in it. She may have thought that his good fortune in winning some money with a Premium Bond had been the key to his freedom, but even she would have been surprised to learn that he had made up his mind some time before that stroke of luck. He hadn't won a fortune, just five thousand pounds. It had been enough to make up his mind to follow his own star. He knew what he wanted to do.

The gleam of the black umbrellas across the long grass and the weeds of the neglected churchyard reminded him of a French film he had once seen on television. Near him a mechanical digger was parked like a baby dinosaur, with its shovel head peering over the wall, the gaping mouth grinning foolishly at the funeral, its jagged teeth dribbling rain-thinned mud. The tracks of the digger had flattened the long grass to where Webber, Mrs. Thomas, and Betsey, with a few others, waited patiently so that they could escape from the rain and leave Mrs. Teasdale in peace. There were no flowers.

"She's gone to a funeral," one of Mrs. Thomas' neighbours had told Andy. "But I know she's expecting you."

He walked round the wall and met them as they left, and she was so pleased to see him that for the moment she forgot the uneasiness she had felt at the graveside.

Looking back later on his entry into their lives, he was amazed how simple they had made it all seem. His room, in Mrs. Thomas' cottage, was tiny but he was very happy there and grateful that there had been no mention of the length of his visit. Without any seeming conscious effort, he soon became a part of their routine and they both accepted him as such. He was, Webber noted with approval, a good listener.

In the days that followed Andy learned a lot more about the people in the village. Webber had not discussed it with Mrs. Thomas but there seemed to be an unspoken agreement between them that the boy was to be privvy to their counsels. In one sense, it was easy to understand because both of them remembered their first meeting with him in Kensington not so long ago. Now, in spite of his ordinary clothes, they still pictured him sometimes in a policeman's uniform with chocolate on his chin. So that Webber thought of him as a colleague and Mrs. Thomas as someone else to be looked after. Before long she had revised this opinion and began to see him in a different light, but these were matters she decided to keep to herself for the time being.

People were curious about him, of course, but he kept his business and his background to himself and it became generally accepted that he was some family connection of either Mrs. Thomas or John Webber. No one was quite sure and, as Sarah Collins was heard to say in The Bull, it didn't really matter which, since they were as good as married anyway. Andy parked his Metro at Webber's house where there was a garage big enough for both their cars and it was this that led Mrs. Thomas to move her plan forward without seeming obvious.

"You could put him up better than I can," she told Webber. "His room here isn't much, and he could drive you if you get a bad day with the hips. He'd be on the spot."

It was a suggestion that appealed to Webber. He selfishly remembered the days when he had been allotted a police driver of his own and it was something he missed.

"I must give you something," Andy said. "Something for staying. I'm not short of money."

"No, don't," Webber said. "It makes no difference, I promise you. Give Mrs. Thomas something towards the food, if you like; she does all that for me."

"I'd like to pay something more."

"Sure, but forget it. I'd be glad of the company. Stay as long as you like until you've settled a bit and made up your mind what you want to do."

It was an arrangement which was to prove remarkably successful and to have consequences that not even Mrs. Thomas could have foreseen.

It was towards the end of the month that the last treachery of the weather abandoned the land of East Anglia. The cold winds from the sea relaxed their winter teeth and became civilised summer breezes. The vicar was unfortunate enough to trip on his worn study carpet and suffered minor bruising and a cut on his left cheek for which he was successfully treated by Sarah Collins. Joan Coley had predictably pleaded for tranquillisers and had been prescribed her usual placebos impressively encapsuled in pink and white gelatine. Unaccountably, they had proved ineffective and she remained in a state of high sensitivity. Webber increased his interest in Ruth Greenwood and occasionally took the opportunity to talk to her, more as a family friend than as a policeman. He became a great favourite with her mother, too, in whom he stirred memories of the quiet wisdom of her late husband. Andy Baldwin revealed a useful knowledge of the mysteries of car engines and their peculiar needs and was wise enough to balance this with a gratifying interest in Mrs. Thomas' cooking.

On the morning of the day that Ted Snow and Betty came to tea, Andy played kitchen maid for Mrs. Thomas while she made bread and scones for them, making him weak with laughter at her outrageous version of Ted's unproved murder by sausage machine in the fastness of her native land.

"Ted's nice" she told him. "And Betty. You'll like them. They're coming down to see their son at Cambridge."

"Flaxfield is quite a bit out of their way, isn't it?"

"Knowing Ted, I should think that's just an excuse. He'll want to speak to John alone. You'd best go and clean up and brush the flour out of your hair. Don't worry," she said, as he got to the door, "John believes in sharing things."

He wanted to tell her that that was what he wanted, too, more than anything, but he couldn't find the right words. He hinted that he had plenty of things he could do and that perhaps it would be better if he made himself scarce while they were there.

"Don't be daft, there's a good boy. You'll stay put and help me with all this lot. I can't rely on Betty, she's a terrible plate dropper."

As it turned out, there wasn't much time for a leisurely tea. The detour from Cambridge had been a long one and

Snow had to get back to London. With Betty helping in the kitchen, his time alone with Webber was short but long enough. The Welsh case had broken very satisfactorily; the farmer and his mistress were helping the police with their enquiries in a most constructive manner.

"You always were a lucky devil," Webber said. "But you haven't come all the way from Cambridge to tell me that. And how is that bright son of yours?"

"Betty thinks he's too thin, he can't decide on computer science or the church. He sends his love."

Snow pulled a sheaf of photostat papers from his pocket and waited while Webber glanced at them and then became engrossed.

"Alan was doing something for his tutor," Snow said. " 'The Influence of the Church on Jurisprudence in England.' He thought our computer at the Yard could save him some library time. Interesting?"

Webber, his eyes on the papers in his hand, nodded.

"It's not strictly crime, of course. Most of it came from the political files; agitators and the power of nuisance value, that sort of thing. Cross reference it, though, and shove it all through criminal records and you come up with some really messy ones, some that I've never even heard of."

He could see Webber's mind concentrating on what he had read and moved into a neutral theme of conversation to give him time to absorb it.

"Seems like a nice healthy lad out there with Mrs. T. Betty will tell me that's what Alan should look like. A nephew or something?"

"Something like that. Lizzie's been feeding him up." Webber glanced down at the sheaf of notes in his hand. "Will you be giving this to the local troops?"

"And get a polite brush-off for sticking my nose into a crime that doesn't even exist? No thanks. You plough your own furrow, old lad. Besides, I don't need any more bumph on my desk. It might just be useful for you, though. We all need a bit of luck."

"We do. What made the farmer's mistress crack, by the way?"

Snow grinned. "Remember we said that at least a sausage factory was a novelty? We must be slipping; there's nothing new. We had nothing on her so, of course, we couldn't hold her. She came up to London and treated herself to a shopping spree and a theatre to cheer herself up. She went back to Wales with a conscience and confessed. Boyo hasn't talked yet but he will. She was strong on God; he hadn't reckoned on that."

"He gets into everything," Webber sighed. "What did she go to see?"

"The musical of *Sweeney Todd*," Snow said gravely.

TWENTY-THREE

In time of trouble Joan Coley had always turned to Betsey. But there were troubles and troubles, she told herself. Dinner parties and cooking disasters and the never-ending problem of her clothes, and stretching her miserable allowance to keep up a decent appearance, were problems which could disappear so easily when she had confided in him. It had never seemed odd to anyone that they could sit and sew together, altering the offerings of a church jumble sale to give her a semblance of dignity. Neither Doreen, nor Coley himself, had ever considered it a strange friendship. Indeed, in Flaxfield, Betsey had never seemed strange to anyone, least of all Joan, who loved him like a brother. No, those were not real troubles. William was different—he was a good man and he was her husband, but even after all the years of their marriage there was still a quality in him that she found daunting.

Now she sat alone with Betsey in his workroom behind the shop, surrounded by the paintings of Mrs. Teasdale's father which he had bought in Gough's sale-room. The air was so thick with the smell of chemicals, dust, and glue, that it was as mixed and varied as the jumble of thoughts in his head as he listened to her and marvelled at her composure.

"I knew he was against nuclear weapons," he said at last, "and I can remember reading about his campaign against capital punishment, but I didn't know about the other thing. I didn't know he was a prison visitor."

"He loved all the publicity against the bomb and hanging but he felt that his other work was best kept out of the papers. Even with me he would never discuss individual cases, not even when the most awful people came to stay with us; ex-prisoners, I'm sure, although William always treated them like family, even though, I must say, he never made my sister feel half as welcome. One man went off with all our spare sheets, I remember. Years ago," she added most cheerfully, as though the sheer relief of talking was like sunshine bursting out from a cloud. "It was just before we came to Flaxfield. I think it must have been the sheets that upset me so much. Some of them were quite new, I remember, all wrapped up in plastic with blue ribbons. I decided quite suddenly that I couldn't cope anymore and I left him—three o'clock on a Thursday afternoon it was."

"My dear, you didn't!" Betsey said, making a conscious

effort not to clap his hands with excitement. "You went home to your mother."

"No, I didn't. Mummy would have been far too delighted. No, I took a train to Paddington and got a job as a char in the War Office."

He looked at her with admiration, seeing a side of her character he had sometimes glimpsed but never seen so clearly before.

"It didn't last long. I didn't want it to, anyway. I just felt I had to make a stand. I think I sent him a postcard. I can't remember now, it was so long ago."

"Peace terms?"

"No, just my address in London. We worked out the peace terms in Lyons Corner House. He couldn't touch his toast but I ate every crumb of mine. I think it was the War Office that upset him even more than my leaving him. It was really quite a drama. It had been pouring with rain and I remember his raincoat steaming all the time we were talking, until it was quite dry and his clerical collar was limp and grubby. I don't suppose I was looking my best, either. I think the waitress thought he was rescuing me, although, of course, it was the other way around. That was when he told me about being offered the living in Flaxfield. No one would know him there, he said, and if they did they wouldn't care. If I went back to him then, he promised to give it all up and we could put it all behind us and be normal and happy together. It was quite an offer, wasn't it? Really a tremendous compliment."

Confession was good for her, he thought. It had put some colour into her face and made her look younger. "So you said yes. Did William keep to his side of the bargain?"

"Yes, William has always been an honourable man; even people who disagreed with him said that. They used to call him a fool or mad, even dangerous, but I don't think anyone said he was dishonorable. Yes, he kept his word until Harry came, and even then he asked me first. In a way, you see, he had given his word to Harry before his promise to me. I don't think he ever expected the past would catch up with us. It had been such a long time ago. It was a shock, but I said yes. Harry was to be the last."

"And now you think that was wrong."

"William did what he felt he must. Now I think he should let him go. Harry says that they love each other and that with Victoria Varley he could make a new life."

"Why doesn't she come and talk to William himself, for heaven's sake, surely he would listen to her? Harry is so much younger than she is."

"You've just answered your own question—women of her age don't want to be thought of as cradle snatchers."

"Well, they'd think that wherever they lived."

"No, there isn't so much gossip when people don't know how you met. William really is so incredibly stubborn about it all. He can't see that it would prove everything he always said, all those years ago. That Harry really can stand on his own feet."

"Surely he would have to get permission or something. Wouldn't it be breaking the law?"

"That's never bothered William when he thought he was in the right. Besides, no one ever need know. They used to send people down to see him but that was ages ago. I believe they used to phone William sometimes, but even that seems to have stopped now, they are unbelievably inefficient, you know." She looked round the workroom with the chaos of paintings but without seeing them. When she met Betsey's gaze she said quietly, "Harry's got to go, I won't have it and I'm going to help him if necessary." When he didn't answer she reached out impulsively and touched his arm. "You are a very dear man. I feel better now."

"I don't know what you want me to say."

"You could tell me that you think I'm right."

"You haven't told me what Harry went to prison for," he said.

Andy Baldwin drove up to London early. He came in from the north, avoiding the congestion of central London, and with the help of a street map he found the British Museum Newspaper Library at Colindale. Webber and Mrs. Thomas had work of their own and had asked him to look something up. He wished it could have been something more interesting than checking old newspapers, but it was a start. He was early and sat in the parked Metro until the museum opened at ten o'clock. In the distance, a solitary policeman bent solicitously over an old woman's head, listening patiently. A good steady job with a pension. Even to himself he found it difficult to explain why he had abandoned it. He was ashamed to catch himself feeling relieved that he would never have to explain it to his mother and father. Mrs. Thomas and Webber were different; they didn't ask, they just seemed to accept him. Perhaps later he might settle down. At this moment he just felt happy and free and proud to be with them.

The girl at the enquiry desk looked at the long list of dates Webber had given him to check and smiled at him.

"He doesn't want much, your boss, does he?"

He liked the word 'boss.' The girl had a good figure, trim and sexy under a tight pullover. Not long ago, when he was still at school, he used to dream about sharing his bath with girls. Soaping them all over.

"Well, let's see if I can help."

She had a lovely skin, it would wash beautifully, but it wasn't what he was here for.

"You could try *The Times* for facts and I'll order some of the tabloids for you—you'll get some photographs and chat in those. I should grab that seat before it goes. We fill up quickly."

He sat next to the woman who had been talking to the policeman. She looked as though she had come in to get warm. Evading the piercing eyes under her ancient beret, he waited for the trolley to deliver his order. Sometimes the girl at the desk glanced across the room and smiled at him. The gurgling of the hot water in the radiators sounded like someone running a bath.

Rutley could not accurately be counted a market town any more, although some guide books still described it as such. The Thursday market had struggled against the tide of modern commerce and died. The town was full of elderly people fighting the same battle and both the estate agents and the undertakers did a brisk trade. It still boasted a local police headquarters to whom the surrounding villages paid allegiance, including Sergeant Burnstead in Flaxfield. The police at Rutley had not always been helpful to Webber. There were still some senior officers there who remembered the old partnership of Webber and Snow. Their unorthodox methods had not always endeared them to their colleagues. Some, but not all. He still had a few friendly contacts. One of these he had arranged to meet in a pub not usually favoured by the Rutley police. Mrs. Thomas had her own enquiries to pursue in the town.

Stanton—the CID man—was huge, with sad eyes. He had once been an athlete but the muscle had turned to fat. Webber had always liked him but marvelled that he hadn't drunk himself out of the force years ago. His capacity for pints of beer with whisky chasers was impressive but he had the sensitivity not to expect Webber to match him as long as he paid. Webber paid happily. It was cheap information. Stanton

ton had not been directly involved with the events in Flaxfield but he had kept his ears open for Webber.

There had been no luck with the Lambs.

"Slippery sods," Stanton said. "No reports from Immigration anywhere, ports or airports. Probably different passports or they could have gone to earth somewhere over here."

Stanton digressed to his pet theory that the painting story was just a cover.

"Drugs, my friend, I promise you. Show me a shady Yank and I'll show you a racket in drugs. They probably use hollow picture frames full of the stuff." Stanton was on loan to Customs and Excise and was rather proud of himself.

"Time was when I thought your actress bint was in with them, too—Whatsername? Victoria something. Christ, fancy advertising piss like that! Anyway, she had once owned that church painting thing, hadn't she? Truth is, old son, I'm a bit useless to you on your Flaxfield stuff. I've not been in the nick much; been spending most of my time on the bloody ocean and I'm not a good sailor. Where was I? Oh yes, Varley. Yes, that's her name, isn't it? Victoria Varley. Oh well, we can't win 'em all. Guilty of flogging bad beer but not drugs, poor old cow."

"They've found her?" Webber said.

"Sorry, thought you knew. Came from your local bobby, Burnstead."

"Have one for the sea," Webber said. This time he bought a drink for himself.

He appeared to show only polite interest in Stanton's story and kept his questions pointed and simple. When Stanton had finished, Webber had the courtesy to go on listening to his problems with Customs and Excise.

"Drugs are a bloody menace, John," Stanton said heavily as he allowed Webber to help him find the sleeve of his raincoat. "It's coming in by bloody fishing boat now—plastic bags inside those slimy cod—and you try sorting through that lot in a force-nine gale. Thank God for a bit of a tip off now and then."

"Good old God," Webber said. "Don't forget your hat."

"She's alive," Webber said, as he drove Mrs. Thomas back to Flaxfield. "Or more accurately, she is reported to be alive and well and somewhere in Ireland. It came from Burnstead. Well, it would, wouldn't it? Not an official report—after all, she's never been officially listed as missing and the lads in Rutley think they've got more important fish to look for, so who am I to tell them how to run their own nick."

"They'd listen to you."

"Not a lot. Ex-coppers are never very welcome." Webber concentrated on the road before adding, "Especially me. I never liked going by the rule books very much. According to Stanton, they seem to think that if her beer advert is still being shown on TV then she must be getting paid for it somewhere. It's going straight to that nasty little agent of hers, that's where it's going, and I can't see him shouting that he can't trace her."

"Could he cash her cheques?"

"Actor's cheques are always made out to their agents."

"Burnstead's full of chat, isn't he?"

"He's got a nice, quiet patch in Flaxfield. He'd like to keep it like that. I could be wrong but I'm hoping that he's just a fool. It shouldn't be difficult to find out."

"What did he say?"

"The story is that she has written to Harry—and what's the betting that he's mislaid the letter? She's been busy sorting things out in her mind. The gossip in Flaxfield was getting her down and she can't face coming back. She's decided what she wants to do. She wants Harry to join her in Ireland.

She'll send him some money to pay her rent up to date and settle up everything in Flaxfield. Like it?''

''How could he expect anyone to believe all that?''

''You'd be surprised. Happens all the time. Most murderers are pretty conventional with excuses; they haven't changed much since Crippen. Which reminds me, apparently she is even supposed to be thinking about starting a new life with him in America. She thinks she might be able to get Harry into television.''

''They found Crippen's wife under his cellar floor,'' she said.

''If Crippen hadn't panicked and run, nobody would have looked for her. Perhaps Harry is brighter than we think. He's got his story all set up, so why won't the bugger run?''

TWENTY-FOUR

It was late afternoon by the time they got back to Webber's house to find Betsey and Joan Coley waiting for them outside in Betsey's car. By the time Webber had put his own car in the garage, Betsey was waiting for them anxiously on the pavement. Joan was still sitting in the car smiling at them and acknowledging them happily with a discreet wiggle of her fingers. The genteel warmth of this greeting was marred because her nose was pressed flat against the window like a child outside a sweet shop and her eyes were glazed.

"How did she get like that?" Mrs. Thomas asked with interest.

"We were talking," Betsey said unhappily, "and I only gave her the teeniest of whisky, I promise you, just to cheer her up. I had to go into the shop once or twice to see some customers and I suppose she must have helped herself. Doreen was out, thank goodness, so I decided to bring her round to you. I had a terrible feeling that the vicar might come round to see if the painting was ready."

Webber helped Joan out of the car and unwisely abandoned her for a moment to close the door. Unsupported, she suddenly felt it wiser to sit on the pavement.

"Oh good! I'm glad I haven't forgotten how to do that. You have to do it terribly quickly," she explained to Webber and Betsey as they helped her up. "I have sat down on nuclear airfields all over England," she informed an incurious child passing by on roller skates.

"For God's sake get her indoors," Mrs. Thomas said, grateful that Webber's house was not in the heart of the village.

"And once in Trafalgar Square with Vanessa Redgrave," Joan confided to Betsey as Webber fumbled for his key. "She was rather boring, I'm afraid. She gave us all peppermints and a long lecture." Joan stopped suddenly and unexpectedly in the doorway, throwing everyone off balance. "It's very good of you to ask me in but I really must be thinking of evensong."

Mrs. Thomas gave her a determined shove in her back which propelled her into the house where she fell asleep on a sofa.

"She says she doesn't know why he went to prison," Betsey said, when he had brought them up to date. "I asked her and she doesn't know. I suppose it makes sense; she'd rather smile and take him cups of coffee. Coley always told her that once people had been released, then they had a right to a new life with no questions."

"And a new name," Webber said bitterly. "He's got no criminal record under Fellows, anyway."

"I expect she'll be furious with me when she wakes up," Betsey said as Joan stirred uneasily.

"No, I won't," she said, sitting up with a fair shot at sobriety. "What can I have done with my teeth?"

"I put them in your handbag, Joan dear. It seemed best at the time. Try and sit up straight and drink some of Lizzie's nice hot tea. This isn't a bit like you, really."

"Harry's been working in Flaxfield for quite some time," Webber said to her after a decent pause. "Why do you want to get rid of him now—suddenly?"

At Colindale, Andy read his newspapers conscientiously all the morning. The old woman in the next seat made several abortive attempts at conversation and then withdrew sadly into an equally ancient copy of the Skegmouth *Echo*. Most of Webber's dates produced little of interest; mainly straightforward accounts of anti-nuclear demonstrations through the years. The photographs often showed the Reverend William Coley in the company of worthy, even distinguished, citizens. If they had succeeded in making enough of a nuisance of themselves they had often been arrested. Occasionally Coley could be seen preaching to the crowd outside a prison on the morning of an execution. He hadn't changed much, Andy thought, the straggly hair and the wild, messianic eyes behind the round spectacles. Sometimes, if the peace had been sufficiently disturbed, he had been arrested there, too. Some accounts made him sound quite reasonable, others were more scathing. He must have had a thick skin. Sometimes he had replied to his critics in the letter columns. It was from some of the follow-up correspondence that Andy learned of Coley's work as a prison visitor.

Just before one o'clock, the girl in the tight pullover came to his desk with a list and smiled.

"These are local papers; provincial. I found them cross-referenced on the computer. Would you like me to get them for you? They'd be ready after lunch."

He thanked her and asked about photocopies if he should need any. While they were talking he was aware of the old woman's glare of disapproval. The glare followed the girl back to her desk and then she creaked to her feet with the determination of someone who knows that the pubs have opened. He couldn't escape her eye. She pointed an arthritic finger at her newspaper and the photograph of a young girl in a bathing costume. Her voice was pleasantly north country and unexpectedly powerful.

"You'd not think I once had tits like that, would you, son? I was Miss Skegmouth in 1930." She gathered up her paper bags and glared scornfully across the room at the enquiry desk. She lowered her head to boom at him confidentially.

"You've got a lot to learn, lad. Don't touch 'er. She's dead trouble—and married."

He grinned at her gratefully and planned to buy her a drink at lunchtime, but by the time he had filled in his application forms and reached the street she had disappeared. He drank his beer and ate his sandwich alone. It was true, he had a lot to learn but he knew who he wanted to teach him.

When he got back, the pile of bound volumes on his desk looked formidable. He checked them carefully but it was almost four o'clock before he found something in a copy of the Cotswold *Argus* and read it with disbelief.

There were photographs, too—the name underneath was different but the face was unmistakeable. It was younger but the happy smile was the same.

"Jesus Christ Almighty!" Andy whispered softly.

* * *

It seemed a long drive back to Flaxfield. Once, he nearly ran into the back of another car when it braked sharply in a sudden patch of fog on the motorway. After that, he tried to forget what he had read and concentrated on the road. It was getting dark.

The light was fading quickly in Webber's house but neither he nor Mrs. Thomas interrupted Andy Baldwin as he talked to them by the light of a log fire and the uncurtained windows turned from grey to black.

"His real name is Harry Brindly," Andy said. "When his father died, his mother married again and they had two more children, so they were quite a lot younger than Harry. They rented a house on an old council estate on the outskirts of a small town called Middle Bassett in Wiltshire."

Andy paused to see if the namc meant anything to them, but it didn't and he went on.

"There wasn't much in the London papers; not about Harry or Middle Bassett, anyway. There was a big war scare with Russia and a sex scandal about some cabinet minister or other. All that and a general election, Harry got about six lines on the back pages. The local paper didn't bother much with politics and they gave him a lot of space. It wasn't a very happy family. Harry didn't get on with his stepfather and the mother took her husband's side in the rows—that was the evidence from the neighbors. It went on for years, until Harry was as big as his stepfather and working for the council as a labourer."

"He didn't leave home?" Mrs. Thomas asked.

"He wasn't earning enough. But he wouldn't live in the house. He slept in an old army tent at the bottom of the garden and only went into the house when he knew his stepfather was working. The neighbours felt sorry for him, too—he was quite popular on the estate.''

''What did the stepfather do?'' Webber stirred the fire and put more logs on it.

''Not much. He helped out in a betting shop but, for the most part, they seemed to live on the dole and what they could get out of national assistance. That was supposed to help with the rent but it hadn't been paid for months. He spent most of the money on gambling and drink. He borrowed from local money lenders, too. When one of his bets struck lucky, he cleared off with his wife and the kids and left Harry to manage as best he could.''

Mrs. Thomas longed for a cup of tea but she didn't move.

''I expect Harry managed quite well, didn't he?'' Webber said.

''Yes, he did. The local social workers were very helpful. They paid all the back rent for him and found him a series of lodgers so that he wouldn't fall into arrears again. As far as I can make out, they paid the lodgers' rent, too, although, as it turned out later, some of them could well have afforded to pay it themselves. Most of them were layabouts sponging on council handouts and earning undeclared money on the side—like Harry's stepfather had done. Harry said later that it had upset him; it was dishonest. Money seems to have been an obsession with him.''

Webber said, ''Did Harry say where the family had gone?''

''The local authorities seemed glad to get rid of them. The neighbours stopped complaining about the rows. The police didn't have to dry the stepfather out in the nick every time he got drunk. Everybody was delighted that he had decided to take them home to Ireland.''

''Draw the curtains, there's a love,'' Mrs. Thomas said to Andy. ''And not another word while I spend a penny and make some tea.''

She made no attempt at food but poured the tea and gave them biscuits.

"Harry really was very popular," Andy continued. "Not only with his mates at work but with the neighbours and their kids, too. He used to make kites for them out of newspaper. It was a pretty poor neighbourhood. It was something one of the kids said to her mother that really started it. She'd noticed that Harry was wearing a very smart suede jacket that she had seen his stepfather wearing. That was the beginning of the gossip, that and the fact that Harry never seemed to keep his lodgers for long. When thc police called one night unexpectedly they found one of them in a wheelbarrow at the bottom of the garden in a large plastic bag belonging to the council."

When Webber and Mrs. Thomas said nothing, he went on.

"Some of the police kept him talking while the others had a look round the garden. He didn't seem worried at all. He laughed and joked with them and offered them tins of beer. He didn't make any attempt to get away."

"There was a grave already dug?" Webber asked.

"No, the garden was long and narrow with some blackcurrant bushes at the end of it. The land had been part of a farm before the council had bought it. There was an old, disused well among the bushes."

"A good deep well, I expect," Mrs. Thomas said. "You make use of what you can find if you haven't got a sausage factory."

"They found them all—his stepfather at the bottom, then his mother and his stepbrother and -sister. Then there were two of his lodgers, not counting the one in the wheelbarrow. There was still plenty of room left."

"Too much of a mixed lot for sex," Webber said. "It was

just money, wasn't it? Money and getting people out of his hair."

"I read the defence at his trial. I've got photocopies coming by post. They made a lot of his stepfather and the rows, and his mother always spoiling the other children."

"Not much of a defence for the lodgers, though," Webber said.

"The stepfather had won about nine hundred pounds and there was some evidence that the lodgers had been earning quite a bit tax-free on a building site in the town."

"And they couldn't bank that kind of money," Mrs. Thomas said. "They'd keep it in cash. How did he kill them?"

"They had all been strangled, all except his stepfather. Harry used a shotgun on him, full in his face from about a foot away. It was November the fifth; the neighbours thought it was a firework, and that's why they thought the children had been screaming—there were lots of bangs all over the estate that night."

"I used to think it was wrong to hang people," Webber said.

"He got life. Coley used to visit him in prison. He's on record as saying that Harry had a fine brain and never had a chance to develop it. He failed twice to get him out on parole, once after six years and again when he'd done eight years. There were letters in some of the papers but then it all seemed to be forgotten. There's no record of the case after that."

"It'll be there somewhere," Webber said.

"Do you mean that someone serving a life sentence for murder can get parole?" Mrs. Thomas' face was unbelieving.

Webber nodded. "On the recommendation of the Parole Board, sure. They're released on license by the Home Secretary. Technically they are said to be serving the rest of their sentence in the community. The theory is that if they're naughty they can be recalled to prison. Coley obviously gave evidence to the Board when Harry's next parole came up and offered to keep an eye on him. A good, trusting fool, and social workers who couldn't find an elephant on a bus.''

''Surely they couldn't have been so stupid.'' Andy said.

''Read your newspapers,'' Webber said. ''They do it every day.''

''You sent his fingerprints to Ted. What happened? Did your famous C.R.O.s go on strike, or did you forget to post them?'' Mrs. Thomas demanded.

Andy looked shocked.

''Not C.R.O.s,'' Webber said. ''They never got them; neither did Ted. I sent them, all right. It was the Post Office up there that decided to call a lightning strike. I may be ancient,'' he admonished her mildly, ''but I'm not likely to miss something as obvious as that.''

''He forgot to post my birthday card one year,'' she assured Andy as she left to prepare a meal.

They ate supper in silence in the kitchen.

''According to the book,'' Webber said, ''the memory of which is mercifully closer to you than me, we should all be thinking of the police—not necessarily friend Burnstead, in case it brings on a heart attack, but certainly the troops over in Rutley.''

''Yes, sir.''

''And they might well get cross if we don't and we make a mess of it.''

''Yes, sir.''

''But you don't care?''

Mrs. Thomas dried her hands at the sink and Andy grinned happily at her.

''No, sir, I don't give a damn—not if I can help. That's what I want to do.''

"You can. I think we'd better try and get some sleep until, say, about three o'clock. Mrs. Thomas thinks she knows where to find Victoria Varley."

TWENTY-FIVE

Webber's alarm woke them just after two o'clock. He had insisted on an early start so that they could have something to eat before they left. They used Andy's Metro because the engine was quieter than Webber's car. At the top of the slight rise outside the village, Andy boosted his speed a little before switching off the engine and the lights and letting the car carry them silently into Flaxfield until the road levelled off and they were barely moving. The village was asleep.

"See if you can coax her into Spinners' Lane," Webber said. "You'll get some cover under the trees and we can walk the rest."

It wasn't completely dark; there were stars and only a few clouds covered the thin, bright moon from time to time. When the moonlight shone clear, it gave the village an odd look, like a badly exposed film with too much blue in it. It almost seemed, Andy thought, as though they themselves might be still asleep and dreaming, but then the long, wet grass of the churchyard soaked his legs through his trousers and the water seeped into his shoes. He walked a few paces behind the others, with Mrs. Thomas leading the way over the uneven ground, guiding them with quick professional stabs of light from a torch, like a bored cinema usherette with late-comers to a horror film. The spade he was carrying made his shoulder hurt but he didn't shift it—it made him realise that he wasn't dreaming. Perhaps she was wrong, he thought, and yet Mr. Webber had taken her seriously.

Webber had always taken her seriously. Sometimes he had regretted it, but not often. He stood beside her now, as they had stood together for Mrs. Teasdale's funeral. Her grave was only a few feet away from that of her father, not lying tidily parallel, but set at an angle, a bossy woman to the last, claiming her right to rest near her father in an overcrowded churchyard.

Both the graves were marked with a simple wooden cross, each of which bore only their names and dates. It would be months yet before the ground had settled enough to support a headstone. While Webber had been busy with his CID man, Mrs. Thomas had checked with the undertakers at Rutley. There were just the two gentle mounds of earth, with more weeds and grass growing over the old man than over his daughter. Webber looked anxiously at the moon, which seemed to be almost too bright for comfort. He was grateful for the tangle of long grass around the graves, which came almost up to their waists as they stood in the little clearing. The only new graves the north churchyard had seen for many years, there because an old man had lived longer than anyone had expected and his contract had been honoured.

And now they were going to dig up his grave. It didn't distress Webber; it was something that had to be done and he hoped very much that he would get away with it. He thought of the time when he would have spent his days convincing his superiors and filling in endless forms for the Home Office Exhumation Order.

Andy leant on his spade, trying to look as unconcerned as Webber did, and was grateful for his quiet, clear instructions as Webber played the torch on the mound of earth above the old man's grave.

"Right, now take this top off carefully so that we can put it back more or less intact, weeds and all, like they cut turf for a lawn. Got it?"

"Yes, sir."

"The earth shouldn't be too difficult underneath. You'll have to get down a fair way, I reckon about three feet but I'm guessing. Anyway, go easy and as quiet as you can."

He was right about the earth. Andy found he could shift it fairly easily. Quite soon it had made a surprisingly high mound at the side of the grave as he dug deeper. Webber and Mrs. Thomas stood watching silently above him.

"Don't worry," Webber said, "we can scatter some of it in the long grass if we can't get it all back. See if you can— Steady! Watch it!"

It was the smell that made Andy reel back and vomit even before Mrs. Thomas had shone the torch on what was left of Victoria Varley's face.

They pulled Andy out and it was Webber who satisfied himself beyond doubt and then filled in the earth over her body. They left Andy sitting and watching them wretchedly, as together they scattered the surplus soil and carefully put back the top layer of grass and weeds. Webber looked long and hard at the grave and the surrounding ground before he was satisfied and they left. The church clock was striking four o'clock.

Andy didn't think he would be able to sleep when they got back. He was surprised, when Mrs. Thomas woke him with a cup of tea, to find that it was after ten o'clock and that he lay fully dressed except for his shoes, which someone had cleaned and place tidily by his bedside in a patch of bright sunlight. The house was quiet and there was no sign of Webber. He didn't quite know what he expected, but certainly not a cup of tea in bed with birds singing in the garden.

"Better?"

He nodded and sipped gratefully.

"Well done, nothing to be ashamed of. That's why he wanted you to eat something first. Bit of a shock."

"What made you so sure?"

"I wasn't. It was worth trying. If you want to bury a body you can't find a much better place than a graveyard, nearly as good as a sausage factory, yes? I thought it was funny when they buried Mrs. Teasdale in a separate grave. She should have gone in with her dad. That's what he'd paid for and that's why they dug it nice and deep to leave room for her when she died. I expect Harrry thought it was a pity to waste it. She died a bit too soon that's all. A difficult woman."

"He was taking a hell of a chance."

"So were we last night. More than Harry. Don't forget, the churchyard is part of his job; people are used to seeing him working in there all the time. He might even have done it in the daytime. Who would bother to ask him what was under the sacks in his wheelbarrow?"

He saw the face in the grave again, with the fair hair still obscenely elegant, and remembered the stench of something Webber had called adipocere.

He spoke quietly, to force it out of his mind. "How did he get Sergeant Burnstead to give him an alibi?"

"He didn't. It was the other way round—Burnstead asked him for one. He was having an affair with a girl called Sharon Ball. He wanted to tell his wife he'd been playing darts with Harry all the evening. Harry took his chance."

"Why didn't anyone else wonder about Mrs. Teasdale's grave, do you think?"

"No family, and the old man's plot was bought years ago.

I checked with the undertakers in Rutley. It was something that Mr. Gough said that put me on to it. The vicar certainly wouldn't bother his head. The graveyard was Harry's job."

"And the mechanical digger?"

"Under contract from the council. Coley always spoiled him. I don't think Harry liked digging much."

"You mean not if there's a well or a grave handy."

"Shave first, jokes later. In fact, best left for a bit, if I were you—if you're still thinking of staying for a while, that is."

He spilt some of his tea into the saucer with the eagerness of his question. "Have you asked him, then?"

"He's had a lot to think about, but he's not dim, you know."

The disappointment on his face, with his snub nose and the shock of unbrushed hair, made him look almost comically young. Perhaps if he grew a moustache—although judging by his smooth chin, she doubted if he could manage it.

"We're not rich, you know, son. What are you going to live on; have you thought about that?"

"I've got a bit."

"Not a fortune. You'll need it when you get married one day, and you shouldn't leave your bank book lying about."

"I would like to stay, very much. And you said yourself I was no bother with food."

"Why is it so important?"

He frowned with the effort of explaining. "He makes sense, right from that time in Kensington, he's—he's like you said in your letters."

"Not a knight in shining armour."

"You said he was a stubborn old bugger who breaks the rules."

"Did I? Yes, well, same thing. He needs a bit of help sometimes, but he doesn't like to admit it."

"I wasn't much help last night, was I?"

"You did well enough. He's not much good at digging, either." She nodded and stood decisively. "We'll have to see how it turns out. Right, that's enough. Bathroom. Quick march."

"What's going to happen?"

"I don't know. I point him and give him a push, that's all. Breakfast first, or perhaps you can't face it?"

"I'm starving."

"That's a relief. Anything you fancy?"

"Sausages?"

Webber walked down the road into Flaxfield, the same road he had taken not many hours before with Lizzie and the boy. In a silent car in the moonlight. Now there were people and traffic and birds singing and sunlight. Like a bright holiday poster advertising the quiet peace of East Anglia. He walked past the church and the vicarage and bought a newspaper and some tobacco. At the wooden seat near the little war memorial he sat down and smoked his pipe but left the newspaper unfolded and unread. There were few cars and only some early morning shoppers waiting for the once-a-day bus to take them on to Dunwold and the fresh fish from the sea. The boy in the ironmongers was lining up lawn mowers on the pavement outside the shop. He'd been promising himself a new lawn mower for years. One you could sit on, with an engine.

It was a fresh morning but not cold, and the wood smoke from the chimneys smelled as it had always done since his childhood. A pigeon landed hopefully on the arm of the seat.

"There's a Mrs. Thomas in Gwent Cottage," he told it despondently. "Go and tell her she's a bloody menace."

Soon the messages would fly quicker than by pigeon. The newspaper in his pocket would be full of it, and every television screen in the country. Flaxfield would be thick with police cars full of the clever boys from Rutley. There would be sightseers and the paraphernalia of the television crews. It would drag on and on until in the end it would give place to the next nine-day wonder. Then there would be the trial to revive it all over again, and then the silly, square screen filled with the long, dreary procession of social workers lying into their beards. The same social workers who let babies in their care be battered to death and the Probation people who unbelievably forget to check on murderers released on parole. Misunderstood and reformed murderers restored to a new and useful life by Christians in the confidence of God.

He sat for a long time, until there were more people in the street, but he hardly noticed them and when his pipe went out he didn't bother to light it. It was a mess, a bloody awful mess and not a door in his head could he open that didn't make it seem worse. It would be a bad time for a lot of people. Burnstead and his wife, and Sharon Ball. He could imagine what the papers would make of all that. They'd tear Coley to pieces, too, and even if you had any sympathy for him, which he hadn't, well, it wouldn't help poor Joan. It would be the end for them as far as Flaxfield was concerned anyway. Not only Flaxfield; it would follow them wherever they went for the rest of their lives. And all because Lizzie hadn't liked a man having a heart attack on Victoria Varley's lavatory.

Ruth wouldn't ever see the money, that was certain enough. Poor Ruth, as gullible as Coley but with at least the excuse of physical attraction. A pity she would be too nice to sell her story to the Sunday papers: "I Was Courted by a Killer." Things didn't work out as neatly as that.

And Harry? No, he wouldn't tell anyone where Ruth's money was. Perhaps he might be able to use it himself one day if he was released yet again. It wasn't all that unbelievable; people had short memories and the world wasn't short of kind Coleys.

"Don't get up, I beg you." Mrs. Fronefield arranged her shopping bags and managed to leave herself enough room at the other end of the seat. "Women's Lib," she sighed. "We have a lot to answer for, a man has a right to rest his legs on a public bench. Lionel was the same. Go for a walk with him in Edgware and his hat was up and down like the lid of a boiling kettle." She found what she had been looking for in her shopping bag and displayed it gloomily. "Noodles they don't have, only spaghetti."

"Not much choice?"

"Choice I'm not short of, who needs a herd of dilemmas?"

He had come to like Thelma Fronefield very much, once you had grown accustomed to her rhythm, she never left you in any doubt. She needed a minimum of prompting.

"Ruth?"

"I shall go home, John, a mother can do only so much. Interfere and who loves you? A daughter on one horn and I have this sister on the other, and living in my own home. Rose means well, she's meant well ever since the day she was born. Now she tells me I'm a fool to myself and living in error with a spoiled daughter. She cooks enough in my kitchen to feed the famine in Ethiopia. She posts me food parcels like I'm a refugee, she waits for the Post Office to go on strike and then sends me chopped liver in a plastic bag!"

"And Ruth?"

For Thelma, it was a long pause. "First she can't stand the sight of him and then it's long walks and meals out. Now she wants him to clean his nails and corrects his grammar. My own daughter, but a woman with poor taste in men, John, her father would die."

"Some problems don't last," he said. "Let me give you

a hand with those bags. Stay on in Flaxfield for a bit and I'll ask Lizzie where you can buy noodles.''

TWENTY-SIX

''Because I wouldn't be so bloody silly as to tell them, that's why,'' Webber said that evening when the three of them had finished eating. ''I don't see myself in the witness box any more, if I can help it, or dodging reporters for months afterwards—that's a hell of a life, believe me.''

Mrs. Thomas poured tea and said nothing. Andy had already learned to take his cue from her and kept silent. He was both relieved and disappointed. He had already been mentally rehearsing his evidence for the central court of the Old Bailey. He was less certain of the legality of digging up graves without an exhumation order. He found the courage to ask Webber how they could explain that.

''No sweat,'' Webber said patiently. ''You drop an anonymous nod, that's all. Let someone else dig the poor woman up again. There's Stanton at Rutley. He's always hungry for a tip-off and he's a bit swift. Or our very own silly sergeant would jump at a chance to get out of a mess and do himself a bit of good. 'Acting on information received' and 'Keeping a suspect under observation,' would soon turn him into a bright copper instead of a randy idiot.''

''And then?'' Andy ventured.

''Well, this is it.'' Webber spelled it out gloomily. ''Harry gets catched, quietly, I should think, with a lot of hands on his collar, and off to Rutley where the boys will get a nice, long verbal out of him. He's a bright lad; he might try for an accident and a panic burial. Juries have brought that one before now with a good-looking young villain in the dock. He might try but it won't work, not with his record."

"Will the police know?" Mrs. Thomas asked.

"Yes, they'll know. Coley will tell them because Coley is an honourable man, that's why they'll know, and he'll tell Joan, too, and then she'll know exactly why Harry went to prison and for the first time she'll hear his real name and she'll listen to the things he did. Perhaps Coley will let the mob take their television cameras into the church while he preaches to us all about forgiveness."

"If Mrs. Coley doesn't know why Harry went to prison, why is she so keen to get rid of him?" Andy asked.

"Because Harry lost his temper and got rough with Coley," Mrs. Thomas said. "Perhaps Ruth's interest went to his head and gave him ideas of moving in with her in London. Joan overheard them quarrelling in Coley's study and Harry smacked him. That's why she wants Harry out, but Coley feels he's still responsible for him. He told Harry that he would contact the parole people if he ever left Flaxfield."

"And if that got the lazy buggers moving," Webber said, "Harry couldn't risk them listening to the gossip about Victoria Varley's disappearance. They might not be as trusting as Coley. And that's why Harry wouldn't run."

"And you wanted him to?" Andy said, looking puzzled and lost.

"You are forgetting the money," Webber said patiently. "There's twenty thousand pounds in tax-free notes somewhere. He wouldn't leave without his money. He might have convinced Ruth Greenwood that he never saw any of it. She'll change her mind when they dig up Victoria Varley, but she still won't get it back. Harry's quite good at hiding things, especially if nobody's looking for them."

"He hid a body in a grave," Andy said. "Why shouldn't he put the money in a bank?" He was quite pleased with himself and disappointed when Webber shook his head almost at once, even though he qualified it with praise.

"Well done—a body in a graveyard, so why not money in a bank? The thing is that banks aren't as silent as the grave. No, he'd want it with him, but not if he was on the run. There's a lot of truth in those old pictures of misers counting their gold. That's how I see Harry. He hasn't buried it anywhere; he'd want it somewhere near him and easy to get at."

"In his cottage?" Andy said.

Webber shook his head. "We've been over it inch by inch. Victoria Varley's place, too, when we knew Harry was working. I didn't think we'd find it. He would know that both places would be too obvious. He's a crafty one, too crafty for that." Webber looked at Andy. "I don't suppose they'll tell us anything more than you've found out already, but when did Colindale say we'd get those photostats?"

"It should be any time now." Andy was embarrassed to feel himself suddenly blushing at his memory of the girl at Colindale. "The woman said quite soon."

Mrs. Thomas beamed. It was refreshing to see the young accept a compliment so gracefully.

When they had finished the washing-up Webber was still sitting gloomily at the table. She felt a slight pang of conscience at his dejection but no regret.

"And you think that if you tip them off the police will arrest him quietly?" she said.

"Nothing's certain, but yes I think so. They'll make sure they have plenty of men."

"Joan is frightened of him—he hurt Coley."

"Harry's not likely to be so gutsy with a small army. He'll go quietly," Webber said.

"But no money."

"No, no money."

In the long silence which followed Andy self-consciously filled the pipe he was learning to smoke. It was smaller than Webber's but the same shape.

"Bad for your wind," Mrs. Thomas reproved him. For his age Andy was well developed, like the young footballers she'd seen on television. "Did you play any sport when you were in the force?" she demanded.

"I was hardly in long enough but I was up for a rugger trial—and the boxing team. I'm not good—but not all that bad."

She nodded thoughtfully and concentrated on Webber.

"Why not?" she said. "Why the hell should Harry get away with it? Let's give him a run for his money."

Betsey had his own problems. Doreen was complaining. She often complained and through the years he had usually found ways to placate her. His workroom behind the shop was his own domain where he nursed sick and broken furniture back to health and convalescent saleability. Paintings were not his strongest field of expertise but what he lacked in knowledge he made up for in curiosity and determination. Open on his desk lay the formidable tome by Helmut Ruhemann on the technique of picture cleaning as practiced by the leading museums and galleries of the world. With inexpert enthusiasm he had read it and promptly reduced all the old man's paintings that he had bought from Gough to soggy chaos. Their remains lay around the room like butterflies whose day had gone. They had succumbed dramatically to an attack of the vicious chemical, carbon tetrachloride. The smell had pervaded the whole building including Doreen's bedroom and the kitchen. But Betsey had discovered something by accident which was deeply disturbing.

Carbon tetrachloride, if used carefully and mixed with a controlling agent of white spirit, could certainly clean an oil painting. But if the mixture was too strong, with not enough white spirit, the carbon tetrachloride would not only remove the varnish and the dirt, it would remove the painting altogether, right down to whatever the artist had painted it on. Abner Gosse had chosen to paint on cheap paper stuck on to cardboard. Betsey's first attempt with the strong mixture had made this obvious. The result had made his heart race with excitement, and to make sure that his first experiment wasn't unique he had patiently and systematically removed Gosse's paintings from every piece of the paper the old man had painted them on.

The paper wasn't plain. Gosse hadn't simply copied the coloured advertisements and the Christmas cards that had taken his fancy.

He had stuck them on to cardboard and painted over them.

He had used oil colours and painted painfully, with his laborious brushwork giving them a crude and primitive charm, naïvely reproducing the colour-printed picture underneath.

Betsey sat and stared at the one painting he hadn't touched, the picture he had impulsively given to the church in a wine flush of ill-considered generosity.

Of all the old man's paintings it was the only one painted on canvas and with a respectable frame. If Gosse painted over advertisement, why shouldn't he have painted over an original painting by Stanley Spencer?

Gosse, according to his daughter, had become like a child in his old age. It was very much like the sort of thing children did.

Spencer had lived and worked in this district, one of the

few places in which he had done so outside his native Cookham. He had married his first wife here, he had spent his honeymoon here, and some beach scenes he had painted had survived. Why shouldn't this one have done so? Spencer was generous with his paintings, he could easily have given it away and it could have found its way into Abner Gosse's possession.

If Gosse had covered up an original, it wouldn't be difficult to clean it off. The top painting would be much softer than the one underneath. Carbon tetrachloride and white spirit, surgical cotton wool and a brave heart were all that he would need.

Unless it went wrong.

He thought of the frightening power of these chemicals in his inexperienced hands and felt cold with fear. He was relieved to see that Joan hadn't completely finished the whisky. He drank a little and felt braver. Not brave enough to do it, but brave enough to imagine himself doing it and revealing a new Spencer to the world. To the world and to Doreen.

There are limits to the courage given by whisky and Doreen was most certainly one of them. She wouldn't take kindly to him giving away a masterpiece. He wasn't happy about it himself. Perhaps Coley would understand that naturally the painting had not been a gift, not an outright gift. A loan, until something more suitable could be found than the copy of a senile old man. Perhaps he was wrong and there was nothing underneath at all? In which case, of course, there was no reason why he should not offer to replace it with a gift more worthy of a church. It needed very careful thought. And meanwhile, it should stay as it was. After all, it wasn't his property to muck about with. Not yet anyway.

TWENTY-SEVEN

Webber had planned it as if he still had police cars and men under his command. Now he had Mrs. Thomas and an untried boy whose only known asset was his youth and enthusiasm. Webber took his loyalty for granted and relied on his judgment of him.

It was Thursday morning, a day he had chosen with some care, a day when the village paused and took breath before the weekend. On Thursday they paid out the old age pensions at the little post office and that would occupy a considerable proportion of the residents of Flaxfield. It was also the morning on which Coley visited the sick in the cottage hospital. Beyond that he would trust to luck. He was trusting a lot.

His car was parked at the top of the lane which skirted the churchyard and climbed the rise to the north of it. Almost hidden by the yew hedge, it still gave him a clear view of the terrain below—the churchyard, the church itself, and the place where the land widened and where Harry would park his motorbike, sometime around nine-thirty. Harry wasn't an early riser. On Webber's knees rested the binoculars that he had once given to Mrs. Thomas as a birthday present. He had already focused them on the churchyard. He wondered if Harry carried a gun in the capacious saddle-bags of the motorbike. On the whole, he decided not. Reading through the trial reports from Colindale, it seemed that the shotgun

Harry had used on his stepfather was out of character, something he had used in blind fury. Harry was a natural strangler, he thought. It was too late to think about it now. Webber hadn't got a gun. If things went wrong he would be in trouble enough without that. It was nine o'clock and he checked the focus again. Out of his vision, and beyond Harry's parking place, Mrs. Thomas and Andy would be sitting in Andy's Metro waiting and watching like himself. If Harry finally made his break they would have to decide whether to follow him or to block his escape at either end of the narrow lane. Webber didn't doubt that he would break. Everything depended upon whether he would be empty handed or whether he would have the money with him. Joseph Greenwood had carried it all in his pockets. Webber was sure that Harry wouldn't want to do the same; he would be in too much of a panic. If the money was hidden somewhere in the church, as Webber was convinced it was, then it would be in a bag of some sort and Harry would grab it and run. Webber's instinct told him that it had to be in the church somewhere; it was the place he would have chosen himself and he had gone over both Harry's cottage and Victoria Varley's with a professional toothcomb.

At nine-fifteen a figure came into focus round the bend in the lane, soberly but correctly dressed in black and carrying a brown paper bag with both hands. The respectful clothing was relieved by a felt hat in a cheerful shade of cyclamen. The figure hurried past the empty parking space and entered the churchyard by the screeching metal gate in the north wall. It was Mrs. Thomas.

She looked about her and was relieved to find it empty of the living. Webber had wanted her to do it earlier so that she could have been safely concealed before Harry arrived. She had disagreed, maintaining fiercely that it would lessen the impact, and confident of her ability to get safely away from him without putting herself in danger.

At twenty-five minutes past nine, Andy, sitting in his car with his driving window open, was the first to hear the motorbike in the distance. Mrs. Thomas heard it, too, growing louder as she advanced across the uneven ground of the churchyard with an unhurried solemnity which was at some odds with the thump-beating of her heart. As she reached Abner Gosse's grave, she took from the paper bag a round wreath of late spring flowers and laid it reverently on the mound of earth where the disturbed weeds had taken heart and were rooting happily again. The engine of the motorbike coughed and stopped as she straightened up without looking round. She had no idea what Harry's plans were for the day. He might be going to work anywhere in the village after he had parked the motorbike. She couldn't even be sure that he had seen her laying the wreath. She blew her nose resonantly into a large handkerchief and trusted that it would draw his eye to the powerful pink of her hat.

It seemed a long time before she heard the protesting hinges of the gate and forced herself to walk slowly away from the grave until she rounded the corner of the north chantry and the comfort of its massive flying buttress. Harry watched her with interest but with no apprehension. The morning held a promise of summer in the sun and he had dressed lightly in an open-necked shirt, working trousers of mud-stained flannel, and heavy boots.

Webber watched him through the binoculars. He saw him hesitate, as if puzzled, before walking slowly across towards the grave with its bright tribute of fresh flowers. When he reached them he dropped suddenly on his knees and looked closely at them. Webber couldn't see his face but he knew that Harry would be reading the black-edged card with its simple valedictory message:

"Victoria Varley: Rest in Peace."

It seemed to take Harry a long time to read it before putting it in his pocket and walking quickly into the church through the door of the north porch.

Webber waited.

In his car, Andy waited, too, ready to swing it across the lane if he heard a warning signal from Webber's horn. Between them they could see all three exits from the church, Webber to the north and Andy to the south and the west. If Harry emerged from any of them empty handed, the plan was to follow him as unobtrusively as possible.

"After that," Webber had said, "we'll take our chance. At least we're two to one, and he'll be in a bit of a panic."

"Suppose he panics so much that he just runs?"

"I said it was a chance, lad. It's as much as we can hope for. Even if we miss the loot, he won't get far."

Two minutes was a long time; four minutes seemed like an hour. The graveyard was quiet and empty and no one came out of the church. Webber's horn remained silent and there was no sound from the Metro.

A movement at the north chancel corner swung Webber's binoculars in that direction. He was horrified to see the cyclamen hat appear round the buttress and advance with determination to the door where Harry disappeared.

Mrs. Thomas had had enough. Something had obviously gone wrong. She turned towards Webber's car on the hill and waved her arms, suggesting, semaphorically, that if she was going into the church she would be glad of his company.

Webber groaned quietly and skidded the car forward down the hill, where he drew up as quietly as he could next to the motorbike. With adrenaline pumping, Webber could still move remarkably quickly. At least she had had the sense to wait for him inside the porch. He didn't try and dissuade her;

even a whispered argument might well alert Harry, wherever he was inside. Apart from that, he knew that her instinct was right. Harry had been in there long enough—certainly long enough to get to the money. If he'd tried to leave by any other door there would have been a warning from Andy. Their best chance now was to get him off his guard while he was still in the state of shock. If the money was there he'd had plenty of time to reach it. It must be at least ten minutes since he'd entered the church. What the bloody hell was he doing? The heavy door was already ajar. He nodded to her briefly and they went in together, into the silence of the north aisle and the nave beyond.

The church was empty.

Outside, Andy waited.

There had been no signal from Webber, and yet, up on the hill, he had heard a car engine start and then the ratchet of a handbrake as it pulled up somewhere just out of his sight. It sounded like Webber's handbrake and the car must have pulled up somewhere roughly where the motorbike would be. He had an uneasy feeling that something had gone wrong or, worse still, that he was missing something. High up, on the top of the tower, something caught his eye, something was moving among the stepped battlements. It looked like a single figure. Harry's figure, and it seemed as though it was struggling but he couldn't see clearly. What he couldn't see, he imagined. Webber for some reason must have followed Harry to the top of the tower and they were fighting. He saw it as plainly as if he were there with them. Where he ought to be.

He left the Metro and ran.

Harry was alone on the tower and struggling to release the jammed door of the wooden locker at the base of the flag-pole. If he had pulled at it gently, as he had so often done before, it would have opened without any difficulty, but it was some long cursing minutes before this dawned on him.

Far below him, Webber and Mrs. Thomas had nearly completed their cautious search. They were in the vestry when they heard the pounding of Andy's footsteps as he ran to the entrance of the turret staircase. The stone tube of the staircase rose vertically beside the tower and gave access to it. A notice in red letters warned visitors that reconstruction work was still in progress and that the tower was dangerous. Lack of funds had halted the work months ago. An optimistic collecting box invited donations. Harry had not contributed. They were in time to see Andy for a fleeting moment but not in time to stop him.

The tower was fifteenth century and the stonework was still sound. But the wooden floors of the ringing chamber, and above it the belfry itself, had been attacked by rot and the death-watch beetle. Before the money had run out, the builders had taken most of it away. The openings in the spiral of the turret staircase gave access to nothing but an empty shell, crisscrossed by the four beams of bog oak that had survived the ravages intact.

Andy was fit but he stopped for a second to get his breath. He was going to need it. He knew that he must be near the top and close to the parapet. There was fresh air on his face that came from above, not from the opening on his left where the belfry had been. He braced himself for a last rush and came face to face with Harry.

Webber was past running up church towers but he was climbing up as quickly as he could. He was still some forty feet below them, too far below to hear Harry's single word of smiling greeting. It was not what Andy expected but Webber could have told him that murderers, even when they might be trapped and desperate, often say the most undramatic things. Harry said, "Good morning," and moved almost politely as if to pass Andy, like a shopper on a narrow pavement with his hands full.

Andy didn't move but the casual greeting had mentally disarmed him and he wasn't expecting to be kicked in the stomach. It slammed him against the stone staircase wall with such force he didn't know where the pain was coming from, only that it was white and he couldn't drag in enough air to scream. He was on his knees on the stone steps and had scarcely managed half a breath before Harry's hands were round his neck and driving into his windpipe with huge flat thumbs. The staircase was steep and Harry had the advantage of the height to bend his head back to strangle him. Andy's police training had been brief but there was a dim memory of unarmed combat. His hands found Harry's crutch and with his last strength his fingers closed over his balls. For a moment he thought that it was too late and that he must be very near the desperation and the pain of death, only the pain was red now and not white. It seemed almost as though the pressure of Harry's fingers flowed through to his own. Far away he remembered the instructor's voice:

"Don't just squeeze the bastards! Twist them and pull them off, you're not buying bloody peaches!"

Harry needed his hands to tear Andy away and to clutch himself in agony. It gave Andy enough time to breathe and for his sight to clear. Harry was still holding himself. Andy forked his fingers and stabbed at Harry's eyes. Then he hit him on the corner of his jaw as hard as he could. Harry fell backwards, slipping where the narrow treads of the stone steps met the curved wall. It was the wooden door to the belfry, which should have stopped him but it wasn't there any more. He fell through the open arch which led into the belfry, only the belfry wasn't there either. Webber saw it but was too late to make any attempt to save him. Andy was in no condition to try.

Harry fell a hundred and forty-five feet. Ten feet above the stone floor of the tower an oak beam caught one of his outstretched arms and turned his body tidily in the air so that the spiked pinnacle of the font pierced his back and his heart and stuck out five-and-a-half inches above his chest.

They left quietly through the north churchyard. Webber remembered to collect the things Harry had hidden. No one saw them leave. Thursday was always quiet. Coley had a Christening later in the afternoon.

TWENTY-EIGHT

Mrs. Thomas drove Andy back to her own cottage so that she could look after him properly until he had fully recovered. Webber was right, it wouldn't look good for him to be seen walking about the village until the heavy bruising on his neck had disappeared. Webber knew that he was lucky to be alive. He was glad that the two of them would be off his hands for some time; he wanted to think things out for himself. He had a lot to do. It wasn't over yet. It was a good thing that she had something to keep her busy. What was needed now, he told himself, was a cool professional mind to tie it all up without any dangerous loose ends, but he didn't tell them that. She longed to question him but she knew him too well. It wasn't easy but she said nothing. When he was ready he would talk.

It was nearly ten days before he was ready. He arrived one

evening dressed in his best suit with a smart briefcase and smelling strongly of pine disinfectant. There was always a fire in her kitchen and they sat round the table with whisky. Webber didn't waste words.

"Harry killed the Lambs, too," he said. "He hid the bodies, then he drove their car to Norwich and left it outside the offices of the hire firm. This is their briefcase. I picked it up from the steps of the turret with the carrier bag he'd put Ruth's money in. That's why I went out to the house. Harry dumped the Lambs down the pit of the earth closet in the garden. That much is fact. It's not difficult to guess the rest and it's not important. Now we've got to decide what to do and that *is* important."

"What made you think of the earth closet?" Andy's voice was still hoarse but improving.

"Killers tend to stick to the same routine. Give Harry a nice deep well or a grave and he wouldn't think of anything else. I would appreciate it," Webber continued delicately, "if you don't ask me to go into details. Just take my word for it, that's where they are—both of them. Perhaps you've noticed the strong smell of disinfectant? At least, I hope you can."

Mrs. Thomas poured him another whisky. "Money?" she asked.

"Oh sure, always money with Harry. This is a guess but it must be about right. Lamb wanted the painting. He was quite capable of getting it himself but Harry had the keys of the church and Lamb would have offered to pay him well for stealing it. Once Lamb had seen it close-to, then he would know it was only a poor copy, no use to him. He'd want to pack up and get out fast. I think Harry saw what Lamb was carrying in his briefcase and strangled them both for it."

"How much?" Mrs. Thomas asked politely.

"Antique dealers must do quite well," Webber said. "F

pecially the picture people. Greenwood carried twenty thousand pounds on him, Lamb's briefcase had about sixty-nine thousand pounds."

"Next of kin?" she said thoughtfully.

"Nobody. I checked on the notes Ted Snow got from America. He was an orphan and an only child, her father died two years ago and her mother when she was born. The FBI is very thorough. There are no brothers or sisters. So—what are we going to do?"

"It needn't be next of kin," Andy croaked. "There could be other people with claims on his estate."

"He was a successful dealer," Webber said. "He'd have a bank account. If he simply didn't turn up they'd get paid eventually. This lot"—he nodded towards the briefcase—"was just his working float, I reckon. We could turn it in, of course—like good honest citizens—but that would, to put it mildly, mean a certain amount of explaining. There would be newspapers and television, Flaxfield would be like a Roman circus. The alternative," he said gently, "is most certainly illegal and probably highly immoral. We can keep it for ourselves. And before you start bowling bouncers, Lizzie, I would just say this. If it hadn't been for you, Harry would have certainly killed again sooner or later. Andy nearly died and I have spent three hours in what you might call the bowels of the earth and up to my waist in something very, very nasty."

The fire was nearly out and she put some fresh logs on it until it burned cheerfully.

"Victoria never had a proper funeral. It doesn't seem right," she said at last.

"How do you think she'd like to be remembered?" Webber said quietly. "As a nice looking woman in a TV advert, or the victim of a gruesome murder?"

"What about the vicar?" Andy said. "He must suspect

something. He surely can't believe that all that gossip about Harry and Miss Varley was just—well, just gossip. He knew what Harry was, all right."

"Oh, but he does believe it, I promise you. I went to have tea with him and Joan after the inquest on Harry. Accidental Death, he felt, was a sad verdict for a young man of such potential. He thought that Harry had a fine mind and a great love of literature. He had been planning to guide him towards Virginia Woolf, he told me."

"If anyone should be in the dock," Mrs. Thomas said, "it should be that silly old fool. But you're right about Victoria; she was always good for a giggle in the Co-op and she was fond of Abner Gosse. I don't suppose she'd mind where she finished up, as long as it wasn't anywhere near Harry. Poor woman, she was mad about him, too. She told Betsey that he was all she had in the world; she had no family either." Mrs. Thomas summoned up resources. It was no time for sentiment. "The Lambs are something else," she said. "Not such a good cover-up as Victoria, suppose someone starts digging around? Sanitary inspectors or workmen?"

Webber nodded. "It's Gough's responsibility. He owns the house and lets it off. An earth closet was a disgrace; it was always a health hazard. I can easily put the fear of God into him, tell him I've had a tip-off from the health people and get him to have it filled in. The chemical lavatory will save his face and in October the council are bringing in main drainage. Roses should do well in that garden. 'Peace' would look nice, don't you think?"

It wasn't a bad-taste joke, either, Andy realised. Both Webber and Mrs. Thomas were quite serious and businesslike. If he stayed with them, if they let him stay, he was going to have to accept them. Money, at least, wouldn't be such a problem. A thought struck him. "Was Ruth Greenwood's money all there?"

Webber nodded. "Harry wasn't silly enough to start throwing it around; he wanted to get away and launder it. Ruth was very grateful. Her mother, too."

"I'm sure they were," Mrs. Thomas said. "Gave you a little something for your trouble, did they?"

"Didn't need it, did we? I told them it was part of the bargain, no money and no questions."

Which means, Mrs. Thomas thought with interest, that John Webber had never doubted that she and Andy would accept his proposition. There were times when a gentle reproach wouldn't do him any harm.

"Well, that's it, then," Webber concluded with satisfaction. "Nice and tidy, with no nasty loose ends."

Mrs. Thomas searched in her handbag, she found what she was looking for and put it on the table in front of Webber.

"I went through Harry's pockets that day," she said. "Not nice, but it had to be done. You two had a lot on your minds, but there's glad I am I remembered. It could have been awkward for us. Bound to cause comment."

Webber picked up the black-edged card with the simple message:

"Victoria Varley. Rest in Peace."

TWENTY-NINE

The painting hangs in Betsey's workroom. Coley felt that it held too many sad memories. He didn't want to seem ungrateful but he hoped Betsey wouldn't mind taking it back. Doreen doesn't like it very much. Sometimes Betsey thinks of cleaning it and finding out for certain if Abner Gosse painted over a masterpiece by Stanley Spencer. So far he has resisted the temptation. He is not, he tells himself, in need of money and, like Webber, he believes in a quiet life. He looks upon it rather like a raffle ticket, and, after all, every good antique dealer should have a dream.

Doreen's air of preoccupation disappeared when she found that she wasn't pregnant and it was some time before Ruth confided to her mother and to Auntie Rose that she was. She had always yearned for a child. She hoped very much that he would grow up to be like his father.

Far away in a bright and cheerful office, a bright and cheerful official discovered Harry's file, stuffed into the back of a cabinet where someone should never have put it. Things had been going smoothly for some time, the Department had suffered no embarrassing publicity for several weeks, no scandals, no outraged newspaper accusations of criminal incompetence. It would be a pity to invite unpleasantness.

She took the file home and burnt it.